TROUBLECROSS

By Jessica Mann

A Charitable End
Mrs. Knox's Profession

TROUBLECROSS

by

Jessica Mann

David McKay Company, Inc.
Ives Washburn, Inc.
New York

TROUBLECROSS

First American Edition, 1973

LIBRARY OF CONGRESS CATALOG CARD NUMBER: 73-79952

MANUFACTURED IN THE UNITED STATES OF AMERICA

I

The train made its usual stop on the viaduct. For a moment the quiet was startling, before faint hissings and creaks obtruded. The tangled tree tops far below in the Buriton Bottoms looked like the Amazonian jungle from the air. The scale diminished as the eye neared the horizontal. The hills whose separation the bridge spanned were not far apart and at the end of the valley, where fields striped into heather, a long grey house lay contoured in the evening sun. The house had been built to overlook the viaduct, and the architect had settled to a retirement solaced by contemplation of his masterpiece. He was less graceful, his touch clumsier in domestic design; the house looked comfortable and prosperous and sturdy. But red creeper softened its uncompromising aspect, and the windows mirrored the pale sky. On the lawn, a revetted wall's drop below the gravel sweep, about two hundred people stood in civilised array: the Principal of the University was having a reception to mark the imminent beginning of the academic year.

Most of the passengers were busy with coats and belongings. The journey from London was long and neat packing had been disarranged. Alone in a first-class compartment two women sat still, looking at the distant party across the valley.

Rose Ferris had put on her coat and put away her magazines as soon as the train left the last station. She had shiny leather gloves on her clasped hands and her feet neatly together, and she sat carefully so that her braided hair should not rub against the back of the seat. The magazines were glossy and thick. They had lain on her lap, but she had not read them. Thea Crawford wondered several times on the journey whether she dared ask to borrow them, but the two women had exchanged neither smiles nor words in the five hours of their incarceration together and the expression on Rose Ferris's calm face was not inviting. Thea had repeatedly forced her attention back to the open textbook on her lap, and after turning half a dozen pages and following the words with her eyes realised each time that she remembered nothing that she had read. She was, in fact, absurdly nervous.

One would have thought, she reflected, that several years' practice of her profession, with frequent lectures and broadcasts, would have provided her with self-assurance in any situation. The University of Buriton probably thought itself lucky to get her. But within the shell of the worldly woman was the nervous and uncertain girl she once had been.

Thea looked at the woman sitting opposite and wondered whether she too was at the university. Perhaps she was even going to Barbican College and they would meet at high table that evening. She looked, Thea thought, like a teacher of some sort, except that her clothes, though dull and almost dowdy, were more expensive than school or university salaries would provide. Ruefully Thea glanced at her own suit. If she was to keep up her determination to show Sylvester, and herself too, that she could manage without him, she would have to lower her standards. Anyway, couture clothes would not suit her future image. She had decided to foreswear being 'the little woman' in every particular.

It had been so easy to see herself and let others see her as an appendage of Sylvester Crawford, even though in working hours she lectured at her London college. She had always been proud, in the past, of doing her work almost in secret, of never saying to people who rang up with invitations or requests that she was too busy for them, of dressing like a fashion plate and of cooking impeccable dinners for their friends and painstaking teas for her son's. The only sign at home of her work had been that she just wasn't there during the day; but she might easily have been at the hairdresser or a matinée, and she managed to get back for lunch if Sylvester wanted to give people good home cooking. Her own books and paraphernalia were hidden almost furtively in the attic, and sometimes acquaintances of quite long standing were surprised to find that Thea was herself a working woman.

'But we have changed all that,' thought the liberated Thea. Sylvester might go on interviewing and publicising, with his inimitable and unfailing technique of inquisitive and searching questions followed up by tactful suggestion and innuendo. He could unwind secrets from Eastern potentates as in London he had from politicians, actors, writers and anyone else momentarily in the public eye. She hoped he would go from strength to strength. Her own new picture of herself as a self-confident, self-supporting and self-sufficient person, a person, in that revolting phrase, 'in her own right', did not include the simultaneous professional emasculation of her husband. When he came back to find her installed in her Chair, she hoped they would improve a relationship which faint and unrecognised resentment in the last few years had a little soured.

The train was now slowing down along the last stretch, a panting and exhausted giant, two stations west of Penzance. The high tide lapped against the embankment and ahead was the lighthouse on Buriton Point, and above it the orb of the observatory. Squaring her shoulders like a brave man facing a firing squad she moved towards the door.

Thea was met at the station by an old friend, who was waiting at precisely the right point of the platform, holding her small daughters by the hand and with a porter at the ready. Polly Nankervis had been one of the spare girls at parties in Thea's early married life, always cheerful, smart and ready to chat, and full of a charitable sympathy with the unsuccessful painters and artists whom she met. She worked at the time for a publisher, but never seemed particularly inspired with careerist ambitions, and had quite disappeared from view when she married a country solicitor and went to rusticate. Thea had almost forgotten her existence, until meeting her when she came down to be interviewed for the Chair.

Thea was rather sorry that Polly Nankervis had somehow found out on which train she was coming. It made what should have been a poised, competent start to a new life into an episode tainted by the disorganisation inevitably attendant upon infants, and instead of the cloistral calm which Thea had envisaged surrounding her arrival at Barbican College, she was accompanied along those long, chaste corridors by squeaks and squalls – one of Polly's daughters was small enough to be toted indignant on her mother's hip – and by Polly's high-pitched and well-meaning enthusiasm.

A flat had been allotted to Thea in the new wing of the college, complete with every convenience and no luxury; however, there was room for what Thea had brought, and in a year or so she would find a house. After all Sylvester might, she hoped, come to regard Buriton as home. As for Clovis – and in her heightened state of self-consciousness

Thea winced as often before at her own trendiness in having, ten years ago, inflicted her son with such a name – he would be allowed to stay in the flat in college at the weekends; and they might travel in the holidays. One of the great advantages of Buriton, she had been aware when planning her new life, was that it had a school where Clovis might be a weekly boarder, and in the three weeks since the term began he had written unexpectedly happy letters. He must be a well-adjusted child whatever his parents were, who took readily to so old-fashioned an establishment after the freedom of the smart experimental school where he had been for five years. And, come to think of it, that was how Polly knew when to expect Thea; Clovis had spent the first weekends of the term at the Nankervis's.

Thea turned away from the window where she had a view of well-kept gardens, and glimpses through rooves of the sea, and smiled at Polly, who was still exclaiming at the neatness of the fittings.

'I haven't a thing to offer you, Polly. Not even sweets for the girls.'

'That's all right, we won't stay. I just wanted to see you settled in. But do look at the dear little kitchen – it'll be lovely when you don't want to eat in hall.'

Out of the tiny entrance lobby opened an only slightly larger cubby-hole lined with white melamine kitchen units, including miniature refrigerator and cooker. Thea wondered what Clovis would make of this after the acres of scrubbed pine in the living-kitchen he was used to. But he would like his bedroom, a cabin almost manically fitted with cupboards and shelves. Her own bedroom also was lined with shelves, as was the living-room. One would have to get some crates of books out of store if nothing else.

This was the easiest part, Thea thought when she was

alone at last. Nowhere was more impregnable, as far as she remembered, than a closed college door. She could hole up in here, escape or hide as much as she wanted to. She shivered: flowers, perhaps, might help? No doubt the heating would be efficient and the water always hot. But Thea was obliged to start energetically unpacking in order to banish thoughts of the comfortable and untidy terrace house in Canonbury. She found rows of coat-hangers in the cupboards, and the shelves lined with clean paper. College life would have many advantages, she reminded herself. She held a black velvet dress against herself as she took it out of the suitcase. It made her look a hundred in this light, but she had looked fine the last time she had worn it; a party in Highgate given by Esmond Smith, a colleague on the prestigious journal for which Sylvester now worked. Just before Christmas it had been, half the women there had been marching to a celebration demo about separate tax assessments for married women, or something else which they regarded as liberation. Thea had been saying for years that she was liberated already, that the subject didn't interest her. It was when Sylvester and Bernard Tate, the Editor, had begun to get excited about this new job for him that it suddenly hit her. Here they were discussing how he would fly to Bangkok and points east; eighteen months, in the first instance, they thought, or two years, and further assignments abroad to follow. A plum, Bernard Tate was offering, and Sylvester gobbled it up without a thought for Thea or Clovis. Naturally to him, naturally, once, to her, his career came first. But then she had a vision of herself receiving such an offer. Could she cross the globe, abandoning child and spouse and mortgage and know they would be waiting faithfully for her return? Could she say that she wouldn't be there to cook the dinner for the next three hundred and sixty-five evenings – but of course her career came first? Sylvester was quite happy about her; they had always congratulated one another on their mutual independence, and after all, she had her own profession, they lived, they told one another, their own lives. But Thea, eyeing a gelatinously bra-less woman, suddenly realised that her own freedom was not such as her husband's. And the next day she applied for the Chair at Buriton. It must have been in her mind to do so before that of course, perhaps ever since the time, before the job was even advertised, when during the usual repetitive discussion over beer with her colleagues about who would get the next vacant professorship they had all tacitly assumed that Thea was out of the running. She had published more than all of them: but she wasn't mobile.

So here she was: Professor Theodora Wade Crawford, newly arrived to a newly established Chair of Archaeology; one hundred students, a lecturer of eight years' standing, an incomplete library and the university's reputation in the subject to build up. Nobody, she thought, could have felt less adequate for the task.

A good night's sleep, on a divan very much more comfortable than the Canonbury brass bed, slightly renewed Thea's self-confidence, and it was an agreeable walk from Barbican College to the main buildings of the university. They stood on the same hillside as the Principal's house which one could see from the train, but were separated by fields, and by a cultural gulf too broad for a modern architect to bridge. There were four tower blocks in varying styles and materials, though none of them was built or faced in the local slate or granite. Arts, science, social studies and administrative, they were labelled on the map at the entrance to the campus. There were large signposts scattered everywhere to direct the workmen. Another tower was being built and more still were planned, Grants Committees permitting.

The Archaeology department was on the first floor of the Arts tower, and Thea did not know whether to be relieved that she would not get stuck fourteen floors up in a fire or to fear that the building would collapse, with her crushed at the bottom, like a house of cards. She was neurotic about skyscrapers, as about many other things.

At least there were no students here yet, which was a small mercy, but Thea felt the shyness of a first-year girl as she walked ever more slowly along the corridor towards a large door labelled 'Archaeology'.

Her department had been allotted half a dozen rooms in this new building although there were as yet only two members of staff and a part-time secretary. Archaeology was only to become an honours subject next year, and for the last few years the one lecturer had been able to cope with students for whom the subject was only subsidiary to their main interest. Thea had not, before her appointment, heard much about Roger Thurstan, who had taught archaeology at Buriton for eight years. He had published two interim reports of excavations which he had either not completed or never completely published, and as far as she knew that was all he had written. He had, she was told after her appointment, a very good reputation for taking trouble over the students. Thea hoped that together they would make a good team, for she was not eager to act as a kind of welfare officer for the young, and hoped that this new chair would leave her with increased time for her own research. The college in London where she had been before tended to land her with all the problem children as she was the only woman on the faculty.

The secretary was already in her room, sorting letters, when Thea came into her kingdom. She was a pretty woman, younger and smarter than Thea herself and with a decidedly cool expression as she stood up to receive her new boss. Thea had undergone a lot of agony when planning how she would behave in this new post, though she knew that it was not a worry which would have exercised any of her male colleagues for an instant. Should she try to ingratiate herself with the existing members of the department, or arrive, as she put it to herself, like an avenging whirlwind? Should she be 'all girls together' with the secretary, and win her sympathy and loyalty thus, or be cool and distant like a female tycoon? It was well known that many women couldn't bear working for other women, so buttering-up might fail anyway. Her trick with successions of foreign *au pair* girls had been to start by loading them with work and then slackening off, so that they always felt, after the first week, that they had had an easy day. But would it be the same with university employees?

She stood hesitating, almost shy, before going forward to shake Miss Blake's hand, and said some polite formula about how well she hoped they would work together. But she was rather disconcerted as she sat down for the first time at her desk with a pile of dismal cyclostyled circulars and duty letters in front of her. It did not look, after all, as though she would be welcomed open-armed here.

'Is Mr Thurstan in today? I'd like to meet him,' she said to the secretary, who was standing at a disapproving kind of attention.

'No, he hasn't been in.'

'Well, I think I should speak to him. Could we ring him up?'

Miss Blake went next door to her own room, to make the

connection and Thea found herself thinking that some plants in pots would improve this rather dismal box – and instantly stopped herself. One definite resolution she had made was that there would be no feminine touches about her work.

There was a faint ping from one of the telephones on her desk and she lifted the receiver. Miss Blake was still trying to make the connection. Thea heard her say,

'Is Roger in, Mrs Thurstan?'

'Oh, d'you want to speak to him? I'll go and look.' Mrs Thurstan's voice was deep and firm, perhaps a little brusque.

'No, not me, it's Professor Crawford who wants to.'

'Oh. Well, he's out then. He won't come to speak to her,' and the receiver at the other end was positively banged down. Thea felt herself going hot and then cold; sweat prickled under her arms. What had she done to Mrs Thurstan? She eased her receiver on to the rest, and said lightly, 'What a pity,' when the secretary came back to say that Mr Thurstan had not been in. Together they went through the correspondence, which seemed to be just the sort of thing she had been used to in London. Full term did not start for another four weeks, and most of the letters were still hopeless pleas for admission by people excluded for one reason or another by the cruel system. But there was no word or sign of Roger Thurstan.

II

Celia Thurstan turned away from the telephone frowning viciously. She called up the stairs, 'It was that woman. But I said you were out.'

Her husband leant over the banisters. 'Oh – do you think you should have?'

'Don't be so feeble. I won't have her bothering us here. The less she pokes her usurping nose in the better.'

Roger Thurstan came down slowly. He was carrying a small child, and was dressed in jeans and a not very clean open-necked shirt. The corners of his wife's mouth turned down as she looked at him. Though he looked such a slob, it was still easy to see why she'd fallen for him, she thought. Those Rudolph Valentino looks, that sexy figure – how could a girl have told what morasses of indecision and laziness they concealed? He had dark hair which fell elegantly over his forehead, great hazel eyes under hooded lids, the sort of mouth which she would have called mobile and sensitive before she was taught better in creative writing sessions in college. All that trouble, all those years through school, she thought, bitterly, familiarly, and what did she end up as? A drudge of a housewife in a small semi-detached in this back of beyond town with a failure of a husband. Oh well, at least he was good at dealing with the child.

'Junior's dripping wet,' she said cruelly, knowing that Roger loathed it when she used American expressions. 'Go and change his diaper, can't you? I'm busy,' and she went back to the kitchen, calling over her shoulder, 'And then you can put him in the baby carriage. Don't forget the net, those people next door will feed the bloody seagulls, though I've told them what vermin they are.' She turned on the percolator and waited, chin on hand, to pour herself a fourth cup of acid coffee. The only bright spot in her life, she thought, and what a pathetic bright spot to have, was all her good American gadgets; the messy room was lined with imported kitchen and laundry equipment. Life was rotten, but it would be unlivable without those.

Roger Thurstan came in and took the dregs of the coffee pot, which, heavily sugared, he drank without complaint.

'I ought really to go in and say howdy to her,' he said.

'Nuts to that. I need the car, anyway. You can stay with Henry and get on with your great book.' Until Henry's birth the back bedroom had been called the study, and Roger used to retire there to write. He said he was writing a definitive new edition of Gildas, the sixth-century Welsh historian, with archaeological footnotes, but after three years the dog-eared typescript was still fatally thin and when he sat down to work he could not think of anything to say. Of course, he constantly excused himself, the subject changed so fast. It was as much as a man could do to keep up with what other people wrote about it. Nowadays the dining-room, in which the Thurstans never dined, was scattered with books and journals gathering dust which neither Celia nor Roger could be bothered to wipe up.

At least the pay cheque had appeared on time this morning. Henry was quiet in the perambulator and Roger paid some overdue bills and thought he would tidy the basket of incoming mail to get himself in the right mood for work. It was all very well Celia thinking he could write when it suited her convenience. She just didn't understand about creative thought. You couldn't force it, it came spontaneously after long subconscious cogitation. The best thing was to go to the cinema, he usually found, or read a light thriller. Then at the back of the mind you got real flashes of insight. Admittedly it was easy to forget them unless you wrote them down at once. Several times Roger had dreams in which he was reading the lucid and scholarly words of his own expensive publication, turning the pages in admiration of his own brilliance, studying it word for word. Only the words never came back to him when he sat down to reproduce them on substantial paper.

He re-read the last page he had written, weeks ago now. Somehow he just hadn't been in the mood this summer, there had been so much else to do, what with Henry growing up to need a good deal of attention and Celia so busy always. And it had been lovely weather. One just couldn't waste it, rare as it was in this country, it would be depriving Henry of his childhood heritage if he were not taken to the beach and allowed to scrabble in the sand. And then he had really been obliged to go over to Pentowan several times, when the car was free. After all, at the end of the last season's excavations there they had been on the verge of great discoveries. One just had to check that it was all undisturbed, and make oneself agreeable to the local people. That was what Celia didn't seem to understand when she complained about his book not getting written, in his profession one had so many other commitments. Not to mention that he had been preparing himself for promotion. He could not have known that his laboriously built up department would be taken away from him; and it had involved a lot of work getting it organised, paving the way, making the hidebound senior members of the university realise that the subject was important enough to deserve a chair and that it would enhance the university's reputation to have one. Not that he'd have bothered if he'd known—

Henry gave a faint and tentative wail. It was almost as if he knew it was worth trying out, to see whether it was Mother in the house, or Daddy. Celia would have ignored it. But Roger put aside the unintelligible computered bank statement and inordinately large pile of cheque stubs that he had been holding, and went out to comfort the only person who appreciated him.

The perambulator was on a threadbare patch of grass. Most of the garden was taken up by another of the things connected with Roger's profession which Celia resented, a wooden shed piled high with excavation equipment and cardboard boxes of small finds. He had shoved it all in there at the end of the last season at Pentowan and there really had not been a moment to look at anything since. The tools would be going straight back to work next week still encrusted with year-old dirt, and the finds bags were packed unsorted into the boxes. If things had gone as he planned, as in all justice they should, he would now have an assistant to see to those chores for him; as it was, that woman might well say that she wanted the digging tools herself next year, and monopolise the services of the new technician who would be appointed to serve the expanding department. How could anyone run an effective dig with nothing but volunteer labourers, mostly weak pensioners and lazy schoolchildren? Not that there weren't certain advantages to having an untrained workforce, who respected his superior knowledge. Anyway, this season's work at Pentowan would make his name, he was sure of that. He would show them all yet, he promised himself, rocking the baby in his arms. He and the child beamed at one another with uncomplicated love.

'It's all for your sake, mate,' Roger said softly. Celia came out of the house, frowning.

'Oh, really, can't you let the child alone?' she snapped. 'I can't go out for a minute without you disturbing him. Put him back and let him yell himself to sleep, will you? I won't have you spoiling him.'

Roger's face was still mild and cheerful as he laid his son down again; he put his arm round Celia's shoulder as he passed her, but she shrugged away and said,

'You can get a sandwich at the pub for lunch. I haven't time to make any.'

'I'm going down to Pentowan. Starting work in two days, you know.'

'Yes, and then I'll be marooned here all day without the car and only a squalling brat for company. Why they can't provide you with a Land-Rover or something, instead of getting the station wagon all muddy and messed up – but that's how your English colleges are, I guess. Well, go if you're going. I just wish you'd take some of that junk with you.'

Roger looked at his wife for a moment. She had good features set in a small square face, and though her dark hair was going grey very early, she would still be a pretty woman if she bothered to make herself so. He said,

'Never mind, darling, there's good times coming.'

'Don't make me laugh. That's what you said when they advertised the Chair, and look at us now. Oh, be off, will you? I want some peace.'

Roger's good temper was unimpaired as he set off northwards. Celia would be the good-natured girl he had married once he got his step up. She'd like it if he became a television don, and he well might with his looks. All he needed was a start, a first chance. And then they'd be on their way.

He drove well, and as he went, instead of his usual cursing of the dribbling tourist traffic which clogged up the Cornish roads from April till October, he thought of his work. It was those paragraphs in *Antiquity* which had put his excavation plan into his mind, just showed that he wasn't wasting his time keeping up with professional literature the way Celia said. There were always useful titbits in the most unpromising numbers of learned journals. At least the university wasn't mean about subscriptions, though there again, he thought, his good humour lapsing momentarily, he wouldn't get first go at those any more. Unless the new woman was so extravagant that she got her own copies. Probably rolling in money, he thought, with her husband jumping on every profitable and publicised bandwagon that came along. They shouldn't let these women keep the bread out of working-men's mouths, not when men had families to support and provide security for.

Pentowan was on the north coast, several miles to the east of Buriton, so that Roger made his way diagonally across the Land's End peninsula, cleverly avoiding the busiest tourist routes. Now, towards the end of the season, most people were going home, and there were cars full of families trailing their caravans and dinghies aiming for the industrial Midlands. Usually Roger was overcome by paroxysms of irritation at the sight of them, but today he was too much looking forward to what he would see and do at Pentowan, and he hummed tunelessly as he edged his way along.

III

Rose Ferris had been glancing at Thea from time to time the whole journey. She must be, Rose concluded, some member of a county family travelling down from a shopping trip in London. Rose wondered whether she should introduce herself as Miss Trevanion Ferris of Penmare. No doubt there had been some speculation locally as to when she would arrive and presumably she could expect a series of calls and invitations from her neighbours during the course of the winter. She had had her own cards engraved already, and she felt a positively gastric thrill, a twitter of the stomach, at the thought of the chaste white pasteboard lying on a shining salver, in the outstretched hands of her neighbours' butlers. It was wonderful to be taking possession. Such a long time, so many years, that she had waited.

The famous train did not seem to have changed in the least, since the last time she had travelled westwards. All these years she had remembered the glamour of its cream and chocolate paint, the starched antimacassars they gave the first-class passengers, the thick tobacco smell of the third-class coaches. Actually, the seats in this first-class compartment were disappointing, not the soft deep nests which they had looked like then. She remembered that when she had travelled down as a child, put on the train at Paddington by her mother, shamed by being given into the charge of the kindest-looking elderly lady in the compartment, she had always wished to have a quick sit down in one of those rich seats, just to see if there was all that much difference. But she had always been too self-conscious, as though third-class was emblazoned on her coat. And sometimes she had gone down by night, and then the snug little first-class compartments with their sheets and scarlet blankets looked more plutocratic and enviable than ever. Third-class sleepers were quite good enough for children. In those days the third-class were four to a compartment, with hard bunks provided with one scratchy rug. There was always a cougher to prevent one sleeping, and once there had been an elderly man, who smoked and hawked all night. She had promised herself then, that if she ever was independent, she would spend her last penny on travelling first-class. These days she was more independent than she liked, and it was not her last penny, not by any means now, and the first-class seats were disappointing. Perhaps a bottle of wine with lunch would cheer her up. She had risen at the waiter's call, marking her seat with the *Daily Telegraph*, and smoothing her gloves. I'll be haughty to the waiter, she thought, and he'll see that I'm somebody who matters. Perhaps he'll think I am a VIP, and wonder if my face will be in tomorrow's paper. Perhaps I'll talk about my chauffeur; and say that the Rolls will be there to meet me of course. She settled her features into a proud expression, eyebrows slightly raised, and set off down the swaying corridor.

The food was a disappointment; it was a comfort that the landscape at least seemed unchanged. About here must be the place where the glass had shattered, that time she had travelled up by train alone, and a small boy's stone had hit the window of their compartment. The guard had been terribly suspicious at first. Looking back, she supposed that he must have thought that she had done it for fun herself, for a lark. But she had been too naïve to realise that. It never occurred to her that anyone could imagine her to be that sort of destructive kid, and of course when the guard heard her name he must have recognised it. Rose had always enjoyed giving her name to people in Cornwall, as though it was a password. It was nice to feel that you were part of the place. In taking possession of Pentowan she felt as though she were coming home to her rightful position, as though those years teaching had been an exile. She had never fitted into that world.

Perhaps they were still talking about her, back there in the staff room. After-dinner coffee time; Miss Finnemore would be pouring out, slopping the milk with her shaking hand, determined not to relinquish it though it was a tiresome chore. There were duties as well as privileges, once one was second mistress, my dear, she always said. Rose would back away from her coffee-laden breath, and carry her cup off to the annexe. The younger teachers usually gathered there, and smoked where the old cats would not be visible, coughing and wrinkling their noses. She was glad to escape from that too. She had never felt akin either to the pretty ones, who were obviously planning to give this up for their husbands and children as soon as possible, or with the career teachers, always reading *New Education* and discussing modern techniques. Rose Ferris didn't much like children and didn't much like teaching. When she left the school gates behind her, she was finished with the problems for the day. Thank goodness there were too few classical specialists at that place for her to have to do much marking and preparation at home. Now the Domestic Science teacher, Mrs Green, she was overworked. But then she loved teaching. She had asked Rose once why she had taken it up. But the answer was too obvious to admit to. After all, what else was there for a classics graduate to do?

Rose Ferris shuddered, and reached for the folded bill.

Monstrously expensive, and the lunch had been bad and pretentious. But she would pay for it without a qualm, and tip the waiter knowing that she had more money than he had, and it was heaven to remember that the depressing career she had adopted *faute de mieux* was over, long before she could have possibly hoped to earn a pension.

The train stopped, hissing and creaking, at Plymouth. In a moment she would be in Cornwall again, across the Tamar. A familiar excitement caught at her. For an instant, she felt a child again, going back to Pentowan for the holidays, looking forward, instead of always looking back.

In retrospect, of course, Pentowan was a survival, even then. Goodness knows what it would be like now, it surely could not be quite unchanged. She would restore its glory soon, of course. Aunt Victoria had lived there all her life, the youngest of a large family. All the others had gone; Albert to sea, to die at Jutland; Alfred had become a Mine Captain in Australia before he died, Julia had married a man who made shoes in the midlands, for manufacturing was acceptable, but Emily had gone beyond the pale, marrying a man who owned a chain of ironmongers' shops. That was trade, and the Trevanion family had never had anything to do with trade. There had been two boys who died in infancy, Amelia, who was killed in an early car accident and Victoria, who was the succour of her aged parents until she herself was middle aged. And of course, Laura, who was Rose's mother, and had done well for herself by marrying a rising young man at the Bar, whom she met when he came to Penmare for a reading holiday with their cousin Edley Brooks. But Vivian Ferris had not succeeded at the Bar. When he took silk his practice quite fell off, and actually it was as well for his pride that an autumn pneumonia had carried him off before he had to admit to himself that he was a failure. Laura and Rose had been very snug together. Laura worked in an advertising agency, and Rose went to school near their little mansion flat in St John's Wood. In the holidays, Rose was sent down to stay with Aunt Victoria until her mother could get some time off to spend with her.

They were the oddest contrast, those two sisters. Laura had dedicated herself to the spirit of modernity. As the fashion changed year by year, she followed it. One season none of her skirts came below her knees, the next they trailed on the ground. She smoked, drank and had boyfriends, so discreetly that even now Rose did not know whether they had been more than 'good friends'. Rose was encouraged to swot, as they called it. It was a great disadvantage to Laura that she was totally uneducated, and she was determined that Rose should not be held back in the same way. Laura's stories of the incompetence and ignorance of the Trevanion family's governess were intended to be hair-raising, but compared with her descriptions of the extra-curricular part of her childhood were very dull. Regulations had relaxed, during the Great War, for the children who were left at home, and Laura and Victoria had had a freedom they could never have dreamt of ten years before. Laura thrived on it, but Victoria was not a true child of her age, even then. She wore her stays without complaint, when Laura tore hers off day after day; Victoria did needlework and rolled bandages, and knitted competent balaclava helmets in assorted colours for our brave boys at the front. Laura had been too busy planning her escape to have time for that.

Victoria was a throwback, really, Rose Ferris decided. After all, she wasn't so old, only sixty-three when she died, which nowadays was young. Yet she dressed like a very dignified, aged lady, rather in the style of the late Queen Mary, and expected to be treated like one, to be called madam by her two gardeners and two maids, and to be driven in dignity in the back of her very upright car. Rose remembered that even during the last war she had achieved this, and an aged coachman long retired had come to drive her about in her pony trap. She couldn't have been much older than I am now, Rose realised, and yet she had the air of a fossil. She had not done any of the things which her neighbours had undertaken, no WVS work, or civil defence organisation, but had pottered around in her own way ignoring anything so ill-bred as the war. When Rose had gone to stay it had been like stepping out of the world, into a time bubble, where the golden days of Edward were lovingly preserved.

Once she had overheard Lady Clementine Grenville, the local *grande dame*, laughing about it to a friend in the village shop and had quickly stifled her own feeling of insult, that Lady Clementine should find her aunt a joke. After all, Lady Clementine was sure to know what she was talking about, Aunt Victoria probably was a little ridiculous. Rose had thought about her aunt in a different way after that.

Sitting in a comfortable train, twenty years later, Rose again felt the little frisson of shame which had moved her then. Shame that Lady Clementine should say that about Aunt Victoria, yes, but worse shame that her aunt should merit the saying of it. But one could forgive it, in retrospect. She must have been going slowly mad, even then, for later on she was quite out of her mind.

There was nobody to feel sorry for Rose as she stood at the terminus, but she deserved pity. She had stepped off the train feeling like an exiled heir returning to her throne, but euphoria ebbed away as she stood unmet and unnoticed and at last she was obliged to queue for a taxi; even that took forty minutes and then the driver was far from pleased at the long drive ahead of him and had to be promised double fares on account of the return journey.

Nor was there anyone to greet her at Pentowan. It was as well that the lawyer had sent a key, for the house was locked and shuttered and it was clear that the former servants had hardly been there since Aunt Victoria's death. The doormat was piled high with second-class mail but there were no personal letters for Rose, nothing to indicate that she had been expected or awaited, and she felt dismal and forlorn as she stood at last on her own doormat, alone.

For the moment she left her suitcases in the porch. They were still the shabby cheap ones she had had since she was a student. It was one thing that it had not seemed worth replacing with her legacy money since she had no intention of travelling from Pentowan for a long time to come, if ever.

The front door opened on to a passage which ran to the back of the house; it was tiled in a pattern of beige and grey, and lit by a stained-glass window half-way up the stairs which Rose now recognised to be an elegant art nouveau design. The last time she was there she had despised it as an ugly and bourgeois survival but her taste had been educated since. And in a way, she felt that it would be sacrilege to make any major changes at Pentowan. It had represented paradise to her for so long.

It was extremely cold in the house, and though Rose knew the place so intimately it took her a long time to track down the main switch for the electricity in a meter cupboard, and even then she found only a few small, old electric fires. There were radiators in every room, behind grilles in the living-rooms but uncovered elsewhere, massive fluted lumps of cast iron placed apparently at random throughout the house. It must have been one of the earliest central heating systems in the county but Rose had not the faintest idea how to operate it. She had just taken their heat for granted when she stayed there as a girl, and remembered sitting on the one in her own bedroom for hours reading turn-of-the-century school stories and courting the disagreeable minor ailments which she endured nowadays because she was embarrassed to mention them to her doctor.

Though the house might have been cosy with a large family living in it, Rose began to wonder now how much her memories were coloured with childish blindness. The downstairs rooms were all painted grey except for the kitchen which was a dirty lettuce green, and in the drawing-room a square of thin carpet was surrounded by splintering, stained boards. The furniture must have dated from just before the First War and was upholstered in brown; there were some amateur watercolours of flowers on the walls, and a pair of china candlesticks on the mantlepiece. Rose put her bag down on the sofa, but hunched into her coat as she continued her tour of the house. Nowhere was more cheerful, not the dining-room, unused for many years, nor the bedrooms, each with a stripped mahogany bedstead and blocked up fireplace, nor the antique bathroom, where cracked linoleum surrounded a stained bath and a lavatory which flushing only refilled with brownish water.

The one room which had any vestige of comfort had been Aunt Victoria's. During these last years of her madness, it had reverted to a nursery cosiness, and there was a turkey carpet and a paisley tablecloth, and a brass fire-guard hooked around the grate. The doctor had said she was reliving her childhood. It did nobody any harm, he said, and she was too young for it to be called senile decay. She was simply out of her mind. But she was really in her mind, Rose thought, the mind of the obedient child she once had been. She called her maid Nurse, and expected her hair to be combed into the corkscrew ringlets of her youth, and to be praised for keeping her pinafore clean.

They were all very fond of Miss Victoria, Emmy told Rose last time she came down to visit, ten years ago now, and they would thank Miss Ferris not to come upsetting the poor lady and trying to make her realise that she was living in a dead world.

'It would be a good thing if we all did as little harm to others as she does, miss,' said Emmy firmly. 'You leave us be.'

And now Emmy and Maud had retired to the village to live, the richer by a thousand pounds and quite unwilling to work at Pentowan for Miss Ferris. It was a big house to manage without help. The solicitor had been astonished when she insisted on keeping it. It was Mr Nankervis from Buriton, whose firm had handled the Trevanion family affairs for a century, who had been the executor of Aunt Victoria's affairs, and had, much to Rose's annoyance, sold off all the remaining land except for the garden to meet death duties; he wanted the house to go too, to complete the estate; apparently the purchasers were anxious to acquire the whole lot. But it had been Rose's ambition all her life to live at Pentowan. The prospect of doing so had kept her going, these last years teaching bored chits. At last, Miss Trevanion Ferris had come home.

It did not take Rose long to settle herself in at Pentowan. Her experience of adult life had not given her the habit of cosiness and she did not intend to use more than a bedroom and a living-room at first. The kitchen, admittedly, was daunting. Acres of red-tiled floor, of pock-marked surfaces, and an intractable Cornish range were more than one woman unused to domesticity could cope with. Rose remembered it as a cave of warmth and snugness in her youth, the floor polished, the stove black-leaded with gleaming brass ornaments, and always people sitting and standing around – it had been the liveliest part of the house. Now Rose made do with a paraffin stove in the scullery, where there was a sink with dripping tap and a cold larder. It looked, she felt, a little pathetic with her half pint of milk and quarter pound of butter lonely on the slate shelves, but next year she might have rows of jams and chutneys as she remembered there should be. She made her living centre in what had been called the smoking room, ever since the paterfamilias had used it for post-prandial sleep aeons before. More recently it had changed its purpose. Before returning to childhood, Victoria had spiced her dignity with piety, and as well as forcing the Rector to hold early services at which she was the only worshipper and burdening him with her blameless confessions she had established a centre of domestic holiness in that previously most secular of rooms. There was still a small oak prie-dieu and a shelf of devotional literature, but the religious statues and relics Rose recalled had gone, and she replaced the prie-dieu with a revolving bookcase from the best spare bedroom and the stools with some upholstered chairs.

It was not so much the doing as the deciding what to do that took any time at all, and there was a certain amount of inevitable dusting and polishing. There was always sand in the house, even when the doors and windows had been closed for weeks. It crept in through the cracks in the floorboards and seeped under the doors. Wherever she walked, her feet grated on the hard floor against the sand.

She wondered whether it would engulf the house one

day. That looming dune, beyond the garden wall, was an ever-present reminder that even Pentowan was vulnerable. There was a whole village buried near by, some people said. Once, when she was a little girl, Batty Phillips brought in some bones which he had found in a rabbit hole.

Rose remembered them clearly. They had lain in the kitchen on this same scrubbed table, and Cook and Maud had fingered them gingerly.

'It's not a rabbit, anyway,' Cook said. But Batty had laughed.

'That's no rabbit, sure enough. Look at the size of it, then.'

'May be that it's a cow, then. 'Tis big enough for that,' said Cook.

Maud laid some of the bones lengthways, and put her brawny arm down beside them.

'That's a person, for sure,' she said. 'Do you look at the size of it, then, it fits to mine like a yard-stick.'

And the next day Batty came in with a bulge under his hairy jersey. They all watched him carefully extract his find. It was a skull, toothless and crumbling. Cook crossed herself, and Maud screamed, but Batty held it lovingly, and talked to the blind bones. That was the time they took him away to Bodmin asylum, and his caravan stood empty for months. Rose remembered the shuttered window, and the weeds that grew over his little flower-beds. She remembered too that the Rector had to come, and see the sad remains. It was Mr Mallaby then, one of the last of the hunting parsons, and he had shoved the skeleton into a carpet-bag brought down from the attic by Aunt Victoria. Rose watched him read the service of burial over them the next day; Christian ritual, but on unconsecrated ground, just in case. They had put him beside the dead Vicarage dogs, outside the churchyard wall.

On her second day at Pentowan, Rose walked down to the village in the hope of being welcomed by somebody, but it had changed since her youth and even when she introduced herself to the couple who ran the village store she was met with civil but unmistakable lack of interest. The small shop which she remembered, lined with liquorice strings and dish-cloths and other unrelated and obsolete items, was now replaced by a mini-supermarket; they would not allow customers to have accounts, nor did they deliver, she was told. Half the cottages in the village were empty for most of the year now, used only for holidays by people who came down from London and the Midlands. There was not even a vicar any more. The parish was run with two other neighbouring ones by a young man who wore no dog-collar and as far as could be seen from the notices in the church porch, held a service every third Sunday in Pentowan. The church itself was kept locked, and its graveyard had received no bodies for years; the villagers, including presumably Aunt Victoria, were now interred in what had been a field half-way along the road to the next village.

Rose walked along to pay pious respects and had some trouble finding the field. A tiny notice obscured by blackberries protected the sensibilities of life-seeking tourists.

Another less attractive feature of life in Cornwall which Rose had forgotten was the rain. Surely it had never rained like this when she was a child? Thin, invisible moisture or drenching painful showers filled two solid days during which Rose forced herself to sort linen and turn out cupboards full of depressing mementoes of a more crowded youth. She actually found herself thinking that she might buy herself a transistor radio, though she had promised herself never to have to hear one again when she shook the dust of Attwood School off her feet.

At last one evening, after an eternity of rain, the sky began to clear. There were slugs on the grass around the edge of the concrete, bathing in the rainwater. Rose stepped around each one and went out through the gate in the wall. It was still the same gate, studded with rusty nails, and with all the green paint flaked off it now, but the twist of the wrist to turn the heart-shaped handle was a knack she still remembered, and the little heave necessary to lift it over the cobbled sill.

It was agreeable to walk in the dunes after a fall of rain, when the sand was too damp to be blown into one's eyes. Her soft shoes made little prints on the ground, as she followed the familiar route, and the marram grass prickled its sharp points through her stockings, just as she remembered. The dunes were changed though, local people always said that they were never the same from year to year. The old sand-pit where one used to picnic was gone now, its once sheltered hollow exposed to the sea, a brilliant green freckled with white. From here, on the seaward side of the big dune, only sand and surf could be seen. One might be miles from any human haunt. Larks were singing, invisibly high in the sky, and the familiar noise of the breakers was a permanent background heartbeat. The rabbits had come back to the district. There had been a few years without them, after the myxomatosis, but Rose could never remember the grass at Pentowan without little heaps of pea-like droppings, and the need to walk carefully lest one should twist an ankle in a burrow.

Out of the dunes and down to the smooth beach, the wind whipping at her skirt, and her hair; it was deserted just now as it had been always in her youth. These days, in the summer, it would be more crowded. There was even a track for visitors' cars, snaking through the sand hills, and a flat place where the churned mud showed that cars were parked. It was low tide, and the hard sand was waved and ridged by the retreating water.

Rose stood by the sea looking back inland. How much was hers now? Once it had all been Trevanion land round here, but she was not sure how much was left after the solicitor's and the estate duty office's depredations, and she decided to go to Buriton and collect her title deeds tomorrow. There were caravans visible on the left, beside the big dune. Rose remembered when she would play in the dunes there, usually alone, but sometimes with Shirley Phillips from the village, niece of mad Batty who used to be – perhaps still was – the rabbit trapper. They used to slide down the slope of the steepest dune shrieking. She remembered vividly now how she had hated the uncontrolled movement, but how, as soon as she reached the bottom, it seemed essential to climb up and do it just once more. The sand had been gritty under her vest and knickers and her ankles ached from sideways clambering. There were marks on the sand now from many more childish bottoms and heels, persistent in spite of the recent rain – worn deep by the tourist kids from the caravans presumably. Did children still lie panting in the sand-pit on the landward side of the dune as she and Shirley had done, with the sharp grass looming above their eyes like pillars against the blue sky?

She started slowly up the beach towards the cliff path, trying to ignore the ache in long-unused calf muscles. She and Shirley used to hide in that sand-pit sometimes, talking from their varied experience about the same subjects which all little girls whispered about then. They didn't bother to be secretive now, the girls at Attwood would have been ashamed not to be blatant in discussing sex and reproduction. Rose had been taught to say, in a hushed voice, 'The facts of life,' and Shirley just referred to 'all that – you know' and they both supposed that they would be walloped if overheard.

Suddenly a long-suppressed picture came into Rose's mind – she must have buried the memory too long ago to recall having had it. Shirley pulling off her pants and giggling, daring Rose to do the same, and examining each other. Scientific curiosity was rapidly replaced by the realisation that there was more than three meaningless orifices, there were nerve endings and feelings. Probably Shirley was a raddled, haggard mother of many by now, she'd long since have forgotten the episode, nor would she be ashamed to recall it. Rose was a virgin and she blushed all over. So she looked quite pretty, wind-blown and rosy, as she came over the top of the sand dune, and paused astonished at the activity below.

IV

Roger Thurstan, by accident or design, did not appear in the Department when Thea was there at all and on Friday Miss Blake told her that his dig started that day and he would be away from the department until the beginning of term. Thea was tempted to stand upon her professorial dignity, and might have done but that she was not sure how much authority she was supposed to have over the members of her staff. When she had been a subordinate herself the relationship between the head of department and the junior members had been informal and friendly and she had never explored the limits of his rule. Was Thurstan being merely casual or deliberately slighting? It seemed more like the latter but she could not think why he should want to offend her.

'Where is he digging?'

'It's his site at Pentowan, Professor, his second season. He was there last year.'

'I don't think I've heard of it. Has he published anything?'

'I wouldn't know. You should ask him.'

'I'll do just that,' Thea said coldly. She went back to her flat in College quite rigid with anger. Good resolutions about treading warily were all very well, but she could not keep an impudent and disloyal secretary. It made one feel one's age, she thought, to think of pretty young women as impudent, but damn it, one had a position to defend now. She typed out a letter to the Bursar of the University asking him to change Miss Blake to another department and to provide a substitute as soon as possible, and walked down to the Porter's Lodge to post it before she could change her mind. She asked him where Pentowan was at the same time, and when she fetched Clovis from school that afternoon suggested that they should drive over to have a look at that part of the country and see the dig, now that it had at last stopped raining.

'OK,' he agreed, not much interested. 'I say, Mum, I had some smashing stamps from Daddy. And Cooper said he's seen Dad on telly.'

'Is he the same age as you?'

'Yuh, he's in my form. He's a weekly boarder, too.'

'Well, his parents let him stay up too late,' Thea said severely. It was a perpetual struggle, or had been until Sylvester went abroad, to persuade Clovis that boys of his age could not stay up till ten on school days even to see their own father on the box – especially not when it happened regularly.

'He lives in Buriton, Mum, can I go and play with him this weekend?'

'Yes, if you know his telephone number, or where he lives. Did you think to ask?'

Clovis was aggrieved at not having done so, and Thea handed him the Ordnance Survey map so that he would guide her to Pentowan. It was one of his useful minor talents, and he gave her a running commentary for the whole journey on the details of what they were passing, complaining at the same time that the new Mini was too small for him to see any views over hedges. Sylvester had driven a Range-Rover.

'I say, it says "buried village" just beside the name Pentowan, is that where we're going?'

'It might be, I suppose. I don't know what period this site is supposed to be but I'd have thought a buried village would be a bit late. But maybe Roger Thurstan is a medievalist.'

'Can we go and look, anyway?'

'If you like. Though I'm sure there won't be anything to see except just sand. We'll have to ask in the village where the digging is going on first.'

The directions given them by the shopkeeper in fact led them to the exact point on the map where Clovis had wished to go. There was a rubble track which led off the coast road, and trailed between sand dunes towards the sea, until it ended in a wheel-pitted space where an RDC notice warned motorists to leave their cars although the track continued beyond it. Thea's instinct was to drive on. Association with Sylvester for years had taught her that those who obey official notices rarely get far in the battle of life, but Clovis was ardently law-abiding – always a shock to his parents as he had been to a school in London which had no rules – and became very agitated until Thea agreed to park and walk the rest of the way. She didn't even say 'I told you so' when they came upon a clutch of vehicles a quarter of a mile on, for it had been a pleasant walk in the mild air along a lane edged with short thyme-scattered turf; the sandy soil soaked up the water so that there were few puddles left from yesterday's downpour, and ahead of them was the sea.

Beyond the cars which had parked at the foot of a steep sand hill they followed a narrow footpath upwards. Clovis said it was like a desert, always one more hillock ahead, and as they came to the top it became clear that he was right once more; they were standing on a rampart in a series of sand mounds; ahead was one more which must slope steeply down to the beach, and immediately below was a sandy and grassy hollow, bounded by dunes on three sides and on the fourth by a cliff edge. In the hollow four people were working and talking. The traces of old cuttings and the strings outlining the shapes of new ones were geometrically clear from above and Thea thought at first sight that the configuration of the ground revealed a rectangular structure beneath it. There was a sort of chalet in the hollow, with an enclosure round it of picket fencing, and a second stare showed that it was a Peggotty house – an upturned black wood boat, with a window cut in its boards and a chimney in its keel. Clovis shouted with pleasure and slithered down towards it.

Thea felt shy as she followed her son more slowly. The younger man standing below must be Roger Thurstan. She had had no idea that he was so good looking, but it did, perhaps, explain Miss Blake's excessive loyalty to him. They all had the hostile expression on their faces of people accustomed to repelling inquisitive tourists. Thea said quickly,

'Mr Thurstan? I'm Thea Crawford. I'm glad to meet you at last.'

He hesitated and then shook her hand limply. He said,

'You shouldn't have come all this way. But still, now you're here – this is Mr Cooper, and Mr Nankervis. Oh, and that's James Cooper coming out of the beach hut. A small boy scrambled out of the door of the boat, and he and Clovis rushed at one another.

'You must be Polly's husband,' Thea said. 'Are you interested in archaeology? She didn't tell me.'

'Yes, I dig whenever the law lets me. Roger let me come in my amateurish way last year too – it's a most exciting site. But you'd know that of course.'

'No, I'm looking forward to hearing about it,' Thea said.

She wondered how she could make it clear to Roger Thurstan that she had not come to check officiously on his digging technique but merely out of interest. His face looked stubborn and offended and he turned his back to shout,

'Keep away from that pit of yours, James. And the other boy. I'm going to have them finish filling it in,' he added, turning back to the other adults.

'I'm glad to hear it,' Bill Nankervis said. 'I'd have given you my professional advice to do so before the weekend anyway – it's a death-trap.' Thea strolled over to look down into a long narrow slit in the ground, about eighteen inches wide.

'James dug most of it last weekend, Mum,' Clovis shouted at her side. 'It's called James's pit.' Roger Thurstan joined her and said in a defensive voice,

'Thought it would be useful to see if one could reach bedrock. But the sand must go down much farther, and as you see it's all blown sand just here, only the odd turf line well down. That's those horizontal black stripes you see on the walls of the cutting. But it must be well outside the walls. I've already filled a bit in again.'

'Yes, I see,' Thea murmured, hoping that Roger would not instantly realise the irony of his teaching her. He called,

'Come on, James, and your friend if he wants to. Start filling the sand in again before some tourist falls in.' The two boys attacked the sand piled on either side of the trench with more enthusiasm than science but gravity helped and the hole filled up quite fast.

'What is the site?' Thea said.

'I'm pretty sure it's a chapel. An early post-Conquest one, stone, overlying a timber one I think. The proportions are right for it. And there have been skeletal remains, human according to the locals. I only did a couple of trial cuttings last year to see whether a full season would be worth while.'

'And you think it is?'

'Yes, I do.'

'An interesting period. I don't know much about it in this part of the world, I'll look forward to seeing how you get on. Of course, there is that chapel site over at Perranporth I believe. And I've read some articles about similar sites in Scotland and Wales.'

'Yes, well, I'm no specialist,' he muttered defensively. 'But I have dug at two other Dark Age sites – though I haven't had the time to see about publishing them. No doubt in future you'll be seeing to all the departmental administration, and I'll be able to get on with my own work for a change.'

Thea glanced at him, and realised in astonishment that he had said that last sentence in a spirit of the greatest bitterness – why, the man was actually jealous of her. It had never so much as crossed her mind that he could have expected to be appointed to the new Chair himself and even the secretary's hostility had not made her suspect it. After all, one had never heard of the man. He had not published anything that she knew of, nor had he spoken at any conference she had attended. He could not possibly have supposed that he was ready for a Professorship, though he must in fact be slightly older than Thea herself. He would have needed a minimum of academic reputation as well as administrative ability and she doubted, after the last week of file reading in the department of which he had been head whether he had even that. Still, it did explain a lot of things. Thea could feel warring in her mind the feminine instinct to retreat at once from a place where she realised herself to be unpopular and the fighting spirit which had carried her professionally onwards for the last dozen years. Damn it, the man was her subordinate. One might even say she would take some responsibility in future for his blunders. She said, more coldly, 'I look forward to seeing how you set about it. Sand sites can be very rewarding, I know. What are you using for equipment and labour? You surely aren't working with two men and a boy?'

'No, there will be some volunteers from a local society tomorrow. And the Buriton department isn't badly equipped.'

'I'm glad to hear it, that'll be most useful for me too. May I look? Where is it all?'

'I haven't got it all here yet. Just what I brought yesterday and today, and what Randall Cooper let me leave in his hut over the winter. Randall, may I show Professor Crawford inside?'

The other two men had been standing by the cliff edge and turned back to the excavation. The older man said,

'By all means. I was just showing Bill where I plan to site the caravans and chalets. I've recently acquired land for a holiday site here,' he explained to Thea. 'Caravans and chalets we'll have, concealed from view by the sand dunes. Miles of beach for the kiddies, just what people want.'

'Really – yes, I'm sure you're right. It's a lovely place. I'm surprised it wasn't developed already as so much of Cornwall seems to be. We hardly passed a field that wasn't full of tents on the way here, even in September.'

'No, I was very lucky, hearing from Bill here that the land would be coming on the market ahead of the rush, though I paid a perfectly fair price for it. It all belonged to an old local family that died off one by one, and the executors – Bill here in fact – had to sell off the last of the land to meet death duties when Miss Trevanion died. Not that I hadn't made discreet inquiries about planning permission before, I'll admit.'

'But this charming boat-house looks as though it's been here quite a long time,' Thea said.

'Oh yes, I've had that here for weekends for – oh goodness, it must be fourteen years. Since my older boy was born. She'd never sell the land while she lived though. This started as a store for my fishing tackle, but we've got it fitted up very snugly now. Come and see.'

Snug was indeed the word, Thea thought as she followed him through the low doorway. The hut had been made from about three-quarters of a fifteen-foot plank-built boat and smelt agreeably of the cedarwood from which bunks and a table had been fitted along the walls and of the creosote with which the outside was kept waterproof.

'All ship-shape and Bristol fashion,' its proud owner said, pointing to the rack which held a row of enamel plates and the hooks from which striped mugs dangled. At the 'stern end' was a tiny cast iron stove, with a pipe leading up through the roof. There were blue gingham curtains hanging at the dormer window, and montbretia and sea holly grew with the marram grass inside the picket fence.

'It's perfectly charming,' Thea exclaimed.

'Yes, we like it. Not that my wife sleeps here often these days – says she's getting too old to do without sanitation. We have a rainwater butt but nothing else. I love the place, you know. Sorry in a way to think of the visitors coming so close when I've got the caravan park going but we can't be sentimental when there's money in it. Look, these are Roger's tools by the door.'

In an untidy heap lay some chipped and rusted shovels and buckets, and there was a galvanised wheelbarrow full of tangles of rope and pegs. There were also some ranging poles which had clearly not been repainted for years and their red and white stripes almost faded into each other. It confirmed Thea's growing doubts about Roger Thurstan; the man was a muddler, no wonder he was still in a junior post. She doubted if he would ever be promoted. No competent archaeologist would leave his equipment in this state for a whole year. She looked at it more closely and saw that the words 'Univ. of Bur.' had been incised on all the tools. Well, she would just have to see to it that they were better cared for in future.

Clovis came running into the hut followed by James Cooper.

'Mum, can I come and dig here too? Cooper says he does at the weekends? It's a smashing place, Mum, you should see the beach. Mr Thurstan, can I dig too? I'm quite experienced, you know!'

Roger Thurstan glanced at Thea, and said, 'Well, I don't see why not. If your mother says so. My own son's too small to be any use yet, but I bring him sometimes. I like having him there and it keeps him out of my wife's way.' Thea wondered how a man could reveal so much of himself in two sentences as Roger had done then, especially to someone whom he regarded as an enemy. Now she knew that his wife was a shrew and that he was fatuously fond of his baby.

'Let him come. Thea,' Bill Nankervis said. 'I'll bring him over tomorrow, if the Coopers are staying here the night. And you might want to come with Polly later, she brings our girls for a picnic at weekends if it's fine.'

'All right – thanks very much. I'll ring Polly in the morning. But Clovis and I had better go back to Buriton now.'

She said careful goodbyes to all three men. Her own treatment of Roger Thurstan would have to be punctiliously proper if he was not to get any advantage over her. Battles in store, no doubt. It should make one's heart sink, she thought. But in a way she felt almost pleased at the prospect of asserting her personality and winning. It would give her plenty to get her teeth into in this new job.

V

'Bliss,' said Thea, stretching her toes catlike in the sun.

'Oh good,' Polly Nankervis answered. They were lying together on the terrace of the Nankervis's ugly house. In front was an untidy but luscious garden, with limitless views of sea and sailing boats and sky beyond. Immediately at the end of the garden, audible but invisible at this angle, was the Buriton beach, still crowded but less than it must have been a month before.

'I must admit I drive the whole way round when I take the kids to the beach myself,' Polly went on. 'But it doesn't do them any harm to walk up the cliff path, and Sigrid hasn't said anything. I'm afraid they'll be back soon.' Thea tried to feel pleased at the thought of being rejoined by two pretty and well-brought-up little girls. But it was awfully nice without them. She said,

'Makes a nice change from Gray's Inn where I go to see my solicitor.'

'We think it's quite a good arrangement. Not that everyone didn't say we were mad to move Bill's office here, but I couldn't have kept up the whole house myself and he didn't want to move. My ma-in-law took violent umbrage because we turned her own sitting-room into the typists' office, but she takes offence at everything I do here, like not keeping up the garden and not running the Women's Institute and not taking the children to Chapel on Sundays. I'm not keeping up the family traditions.'

'At least you live in the family house.'

'Well, Bill insisted or I wouldn't. Though I'm quite pleased now, it's convenient with the children and having that gate out to the beach steps will be a help when they're old enough to go down alone. But it's awfully ugly. Not like my dream cottage in the country.' Thea had admittedly been surprised to find Polly living in such a grown-up-looking house, a nineteenth-century manifestation of prosperity built out of local granite by one of Bill's merchant ancestors. Still, it had the good view and was conveniently near the middle of town, and with all the living-rooms facing the garden it was only the office side of the house which was disturbed by the continuous traffic along the scenic coast road. 'Randall Cooper wanted to buy it and make it into a hotel but believe it or not Bill loves the place, and he wouldn't think of it though we'd have made a whacking profit, even after buying another house and office.'

'I met him yesterday when I went to see that dig. Is he a local figure?'

'Yes, in a way. He isn't a Cornishman, but he came down years ago and he's made heaps of money with his holiday camps and what-not. He's got a reputation for being a bit sharp, especially with women – you want to take care – but forget I said so as Bill's his lawyer.'

'He certainly seemed to jump in pretty fast at Pentowan. It seems a shame to think of him developing that coast.'

'The awful thing is that he seems to be getting permission for it too. The Council don't seem to think the Pentowan area is saturated yet, though I should have thought it was almost solid holiday-makers in the summer. But there was a dotty old woman who hung on to most of the land and wouldn't let anyone do anything although she never set her foot outside the house herself. Some phobia about the sand overwhelming the whole parish if anyone touched it.

Apparently it happened once, like Pompeii you know, a whole farmhouse or village or something got buried in the night. The sand dunes do shift about even now but Bill said that it was nonsense to be worried about being overwhelmed or anything. He was awfully pleased when Randall let that chap from your department start digging on his bit, anyway.'

'But I thought he'd only bought it this year? How come that Roger dug his trial trenches last year, and that Peggotty boat of the Coopers must have been there for ages – he said about fifteen years I think.'

'Oh, I don't know about that. Maybe the Coopers bought that bit from the Trevanions before the old thing went round the bend or something. I suppose Rose Ferris may have something to say about that – she's the niece. Bill thinks she must be bats too as she wants to live in the house all alone and not sell it or anything. Hellish lonely in the winter, and she's not married either. Bill said I should call on her, see if she'd give bed and breakfast to some diggers. We might do that this afternoon if you can face it, when we go over.'

'I don't mind giving you moral support. But I don't see why you're landed with the job, Polly, and the Thurstans might think I was interfering. After all, it's his dig not mine.'

'Celia Thurstan's a bitch – you don't want to bother about her. And nothing you do could make her more bitchy, anyway.'

'About me d'you mean?' Thea asked. Polly blushed, but answered,

'She has been bloody about you, I can't think why you shouldn't be told. It's ridiculous for Bill to suppose you won't find out so it might just as well be me that tells you. She thinks her Roger should have got your job and she's very bitter about it. I must say in her place I would not go round telling people so, but she's one of those women with a high IQ who're absolute nits when it comes to ordinary life. She knows she's so clever, she just can't see what other people are thinking.'

'But do other people think I'm keeping him out of his rights or something? After all, lots of people must have applied for the job.'

'Heavens, Thea, don't let it worry you. I dare say some people think Roger Thurstan's been hard done by, but presumably the appointments committee knew what it was doing. He's the poor local boy made good, which gets him some sympathy. His family were farm labourers – and he went from village school to Cambridge and all that. Then he went to America on a scholarship or something, met Celia and came back home in a blaze of glory to a good job. But she never lets him forget how little money he's making by American standards and what a backwater Buriton is. She wants him to get rich and famous somehow.'

'I see,' Thea said. 'That explains a lot. But they really shouldn't blame me – it might have been somebody else to get the job, but I doubt if he would have. He simply isn't good enough, as far as I can see.'

'Don't worry about it, I told you she's a bitch. Life's too short to think about women like Celia Thurstan. And I know I don't do anything except be a wife and mother but I don't go round nagging Bill either, and I think she should go out and get fame and all that for herself if she wants it so much. Like you, Thea. But I asked her once why she didn't work if she had all those marvellous American degrees, and she said that there wasn't anything she could do in the back of beyond, which is her flattering way of talking about Buriton.'

'You don't think of it like that, do you?'

'Oh no, I never wanted to do anything except be domestic and I can do that as well here as anywhere else. Better, probably. I even have a good excuse for baking my own bread because the local bakers are so rotten. Celia Thurstan just complains about it, but she doesn't do anything constructive. Her brains are too good to waste on yeast she said when I asked her why, and I'm not making it up, she really did say that. I should think she leads Roger a hell of a life. Though of course one would be on his side – he's so handsome.'

'I don't think that aspect of him will affect me,' Thea said drily.

'Oh, Thea – I didn't mean to ask or say anything. But you've been such a clam. Are you and Sylvester divorcing – is this your two years separation by agreement or what?'

'No, I ought to have told you I suppose. We haven't any intention of getting divorced and you might let people round here know that I'm not available. We're just not living in the same place at the moment, that's all. I could hardly have taken Clovis to travel round the Far East, and anyway, I have my own career to think of. I rather thought that we might make Buriton the family base if Sylvester goes on with this travelling lark, it's only a good night's sleep away from London after all. But no jokes about Roger Thurstan, I do beg.'

VI

There was nobody in at Pentowan House when Polly and Thea drove up to it, having left the little girls playing in the sand dump beside the trench where their father was scrapping with his trowel.

The house was an uncompromising oblong built of smooth-cut granite blocks which were ugly but indestructible, so that although the state of the paint on doors and window frames made it obvious that no work had been done to maintain the property for years, the whole thing was not in as bad order as it might have been. Concrete had been spread all around the house unbroken by a single flower-bed, and between its expanse and the high wall bounding the property was overgrown grass.

'God, how ghastly,' Polly whispered as they stood in the porch. 'Imagine her wanting to stay here for a day.'

'Yes, and unimprovable too, I'd have thought. No trees, no flowers – it's like a prison.' Polly rang again, and they waited, childishly trying not to giggle. But nobody came to the door, nor any sound from within the house.

'It's funny, Thea, she must be somewhere around. Look, the door isn't actually locked, and I don't think that glass inner one is either. And lots of windows are open.'

'Shall we go and ring at the back?' They walked around the house, careful on the slimy greenish path, and knocked loudly on the back door. After a while Polly tried its handle and when it opened put her head around, to peer into the scullery.

'Look, how peculiar,' she exclaimed, 'there's mould growing in the dirty dishes! What sort of person can Miss Ferris be? And look at the milk in that bottle.'

'Ugh. And doesn't it smell. But, Polly, there must be something wrong. Nobody would leave her kitchen like this, surely. Do you think she might be ill upstairs? Hadn't we better go and look?' They went through the icy kitchen, their shoes grating on the invisible sand which had been blown on to the floor. Standing in the equally cold and bleak hall, Polly called,

'Miss Ferris! Miss Trevanion Ferris – are you there? May we come in?' But there was no answer. Polly shivered and said, 'Gosh, it feels as though it's been empty a long time. Like a house that's been on the market for years. I suppose we ought to look for her. Thank goodness you came with me, Thea, I'd have hated this on my own. Doesn't it give you the creeps?' They looked into the downstairs rooms, which were all tidy, bleak, cold and uninhabited. 'Perhaps she's died in her bed,' Polly whispered.

Thea was about to make some bracing remark as much to cheer herself as Polly when the front door bell startlingly pealed. Feeling like robbers, the two women's first reaction was to escape, but Thea said, 'We'd better go. After all, she wouldn't ring her own bell,' and she went up the long passage to the door. As they had seen from the outside, the glass porch door was not locked and in fact had no keyhole, and the outer wooden door was ajar; presumably the habit, as in most country houses, was to leave the outer door hospitably open all day. The beaming smile left the face of the girl who was standing outside as Thea opened the door. She said,

'Oh – I must have made a mistake. I came to see Miss

Ferris.' She spoke with a faint London accent and looked sharp and cocky, with too much make-up and provocative clothes. She must have been about fifteen.

'This is her house, we're looking for her too. Are you a relation of hers?' Thea said.

'No, I'm not. She used to teach me at school. Classics. I thought she'd be pleased to see me – we're on holiday near here.'

'Well, I don't know quite what to say,' Thea said. At least this child knew what Miss Ferris looked like which was more than Polly or Thea did, but in spite of her precociously sophisticated air she was too young to be allowed to come exploring upstairs in case they found Miss Ferris ill – or worse. Polly was more automatically motherly than Thea. She smiled at the girl and said,

'Look, I'm Mrs Nankervis and this is Mrs Crawford. We're just going to look upstairs and make sure there's nothing wrong. Why don't you just wait down here for a moment? Was she expecting you?'

'No, she didn't know we were coming down. But I know she'd like to see me. We had such a close relationship at school, not like with the other girls.'

Thea stood looking at the girl, for a moment, transported in memory to her own schooldays. There had been a middle-aged woman with whom Thea had had private maths coaching, a woman once beautiful but desiccated now, her black-cropped hair no longer chic and glossy and deep lines of disappointment on her olive skin; she had been one of those women teachers who terrify girls with quiet sarcasms to the extent that they hardly dare joke about her even on their own. And then, in those private lessons, she had behaved so differently that Thea had hugged a secret to herself for the whole of a school year, that Miss Cullen was human after all. It had taken a first boy-friend and the release from the academic prison of intensive exam coaching to make Thea realise how unnatural her relationship with Miss Cullen had been – those paroxysms of giggles which had overtaken them both, the way in which a purely mental and emotional contact had been made to feel like something physical. And then the term after, when Thea came back to school changed and educated by her boy-friend's embraces, knowing for the first time the shape of the smooth curves of her own body from the touch of another's hand, she had realised that that was what Miss Cullen wanted: she was aching, as she locked her eyes with Thea's from the dais'd desk, longing to feel Thea as Roy had done, to be as aware of that young flesh as she was of the mind it housed. Something must have shown in Thea's behaviour, perhaps a glance of understanding, perhaps merely a forced quality to her jokes and laughter, but after that Miss Cullen had become biting and sarcastic as never before. Thea would have left school rather than sit under her any longer, even without the necessary exams and qualifications, if it had not been for Roy in the evenings, telling her that the woman was jealous, that she was a poor old thing, that her own life was over and she couldn't bear to think of Thea's before her.

Somehow, looking at this chit now, so like Thea had been, in spite of the vulgarity above the pert intelligence, Thea recognised the relationship there must have been between the woman and the girl, more than that merely between teacher and taught. She said,

'Yes, you wait here, we'll go and look,' and the girl sat down on a narrow oak settle in the hall and followed the two women with her eyes as they went upstairs.

But they need not have been apprehensive. None of the

rooms was occupied or locked – there were four bedrooms stripped and dust-sheeted and a fifth tidy and used but empty; the bathroom was clean, furnished with towels and face flannels and a glass of brown water with senna pods floating in it; but no Miss Trevanion Ferris anywhere.

'We ought to go to the police,' the girl said energetically, but Polly said,

'I don't think that's necessary at this stage. We don't know anything about Miss Ferris's way of life, and she might well not thank us for that sort of interference. I'll discuss it with my husband who looks after Miss Ferris's affairs and see what he says. Do you want to come along and see the excavations with us – what's your name by the way?'

'Julie – Julie Robertson. But I think I'm going to hang on for a bit, Miss Ferris might come back.'

'I wonder whether – Thea, what do you think?'

'I don't think that Julie will come to any harm here,' said Thea, who had taken a groundless dislike to the girl. 'I suppose your parents know where you are? Yes, well, that's fine, but I shouldn't go poking around if I were you, I'm sure Miss Ferris wouldn't like it. In fact, we'll shut the front door properly now, shall we?' As she and Polly got into Polly's car, she added more quietly, 'Just as well that she doesn't find a body, if there is one. Or any other nasty thing in the woodshed, come to that. What do you think has happened to the woman?'

'I can't think. From the kitchen it looks as though she last touched it days ago, but then for all we know she may be the sort of woman who does leave her kitchen to get stinking. And the doors not being locked doesn't mean a thing, nobody bothers with locking up down here. When I moved in to Bill's family home there wasn't even a key to two of the outside doors; though they always had servants in the house which made a difference. My mother-in-law thinks I'm neurotic because I keep locking things up. But you know, as far as looking for Miss Ferris goes, it's a bit awkward when we don't even know what she looks like. I don't think even Bill's done more than speak to her on the telephone either. But here we are, we'll ask him.'

They had driven round in a loop which brought them back to within a hundred yards of Pentowan House, and Polly put her car in the patch where Clovis had not liked to go on their earlier visit. Polly explained, 'Actually, the Council can't really stop people driving right up here because nobody knows who the lane belongs to. But their notice scares most of the tourists which is just as well. But I forgot, you came here yesterday, didn't you?'

They scrambled up the steep slope with bags of picnic tea and vacuum flasks. Polly had explained earlier that she had to provide food for far more than her own family on these occasions, although the diggers were supposed to bring their own. It made quite a change for Thea. Usually she was panting in a trench for the shout of 'Tea's up'.

They had a bird's-eye view from the crest of the sand dune of a gratifyingly industrious scene; there were about ten people in coloured jeans and anoraks scraping, shovelling, spading and wheeling barrows along precarious, narrow baulks. Where yesterday there had been one deep slit trench – the pit dug and filled in by the little boys – there was now a maze of cuttings laid out at angles to one another, some already dug well down into the soil, some scars where the turf had been peeled off ready for digging and some just shaped in readiness by string stretched tight between painted pegs. So far it appeared a textbook way of starting an excavation. Several of the diggers seemed to be experienced and to know exactly what they were doing; most worked more slowly, looking around repeatedly for instruction or to see what the others were up to. There were few men; apart from Roger Thurstan himself, who walked around looking important with a trowel, a notebook and a measuring tape, but did not seem to be mucking in himself, and Randall Cooper, who sat on the ground smoking a pipe with a newspaper beside him, all the local volunteers were women, plus, of course, Clovis and James. These two were crouched in a trench within the rectangular structure whose shape was visible under the ground's surface; already one of the trenches at right-angles to a long wall was revealing that the wall was made of stone.

Clovis and James were trowelling professionally away, scraping sand on to small coal shovels and then transferring it into buckets. Thea and Polly watched as a fat girl rather grumpily emptied the bucket's contents through a large sieve into a wheelbarrow, and pushed it away to the dump where Polly's daughters were 'digging'.

'I expect those two little boys know more about it than most of the others,' Thea said placatingly, seeing that Polly's face expressed disapproval of the boys doing a sedentary job while a grown-up laboured for them. 'Clovis is pretty experienced anyway, and the other boy looks as though he knows what he's doing.'

'Won't they get bored rather quickly?'

'I dare say. Though Clovis seems quite to like it. And it helps that James Cooper is there. On my digs Clovis does get a bit fed up, being the only kid.'

'He must become a bit of a nuisance.'

'Not too bad. It was easy when he was a baby, of course, we simply built him a sort of cage, like a giant playpen, and he didn't get in the way at all.'

'Poor little chap.'

'Oh no, he loved it. The girls who dig are always glad of an excuse to skive off and have a rest and they kept him quiet. Most girls rather hate digging really, so cold and wet and dirty. I know I used to hate the donkey work, until I learnt enough to start supervising. But they have to do it to get degrees in archaeology. And of course the younger ones think it sounds glamorous till they actually find themselves doing hard labour eight hours a day.'

'They probably think it's worth the effort when they find something.'

'They might well, if they ever did! I suppose it's different on this alkaline soil, but on most digs the small finds are few and far between, they just don't survive in the conditions. That's the trouble, the volunteers tend to come along expecting a sort of treasure hunt. Actually I read in a periodical that some teachers of archaeology in America run pretend training digs, instead of teaching the students on real sites like this, and plant goodies all over the place to cheer people on.' Thea and Polly started to descend towards the diggers, and Polly's daughters, catching sight of them, ran towards them. Bill Nankervis jumped to stop them trampling down a baulk, and Roger shouted, 'Not that way, girls, please. Bill, do stop them.'

Polly called, as she spread her arms wide to her daughters,

'Have you seen Rose Ferris, Roger? Bill? Did she come over here? There's no sign of her at the house.'

The two men looked questioningly at each other, and shook their heads.

At this moment Clovis called in a casual voice,

'I've got something here, Mr Thurstan. Bone, I think.'

'It'll just be another rabbit, Clovis. The place must have

been seething with them.'

'No, sir, I'm sure it's bigger than that. Might be a cow.'

'Or a dinosaur, you supersonic nit,' James said loudly, and the two boys bent double with giggles.

Roger said, 'I'd better look, I suppose,' and Thea watched him with interest as he walked across and bent over the exposed bone with his trowel. She would have liked to go and look herself, for she was pretty sure that Clovis would recognise a rabbit bone when he saw one. Little boys in her experience were sophisticatedly aware of what lay under their skin. But she restrained herself, and helped Polly to lay out packets of biscuits and jam sandwiches, watching from the corner of her eye. Roger's face was flushed, and a James Bond-type comma of hair hung over his forehead. With those looks, she thought, he could hardly not see himself as a romantic hero.

'I think you have found something good,' Roger said, loud enough for the other workers to hear and straighten up to listen. 'As a matter of fact, I think it's a human rib. Look, get a couple of brushes, will you, we don't want to go breaking it up. Now, who's got some experience I wonder?' He looked around, and Clovis shouted,

'Oh, sir, do let me do it. I know how – tell him I know how, Mum.' Thea shook her head, dissociating herself.

'Well, OK, you boys brush and blow, and we'll get – Mrs Dovey, would you like to see to this?' An elderly woman whose appearance was not enhanced by the baggy ex-army overalls she was wearing went over to squat beside the two boys, and Roger accepted the plastic mugful of tea which Polly held out to him. 'There are bound to be inhumations if this is the sort of site I think,' he said casually. 'Burial in holy ground, and the closer in the holier, you know. Like putting crusaders inside the church instead of in the graveyard. But I'm teaching my grandmother – sorry.' He seemed friendlier today, more anxious to please, Thea thought, and she said,

'No, no, I'm profoundly ignorant about the period.'

'I think it's creepy, digging up bodies,' Polly said through a mouthful of digestive biscuit. 'Are you sure it's all right for those children?'

'Oh, Clovis has done it before. He uncovered an infant's inhumation under the walls of the last site I dug, a ritual offering probably. Little boys are terrifically callous.'

Bill Nankervis spoke unexpectedly. 'I'm not sure I don't agree with Polly,' he said as though it were unusual. 'If people were buried in consecrated ground, ought we to disturb them? I do feel a bit uneasy about it; my Methodist upbringing I suppose.'

'They can be reinterred with all sorts of ceremonies and services,' Thea said. 'The landowner insisted on that on my last dig and that wasn't even a Christian site. I can't say that I see the point of it myself.'

'I do, I think, although I'm an agnostic,' Roger said slowly. 'The place had quite an atmosphere of – well, departed spirits, when I was here the other night. Have you ever felt that, Randall?'

'Can't say I have. But then I never knew there were any here until you told me so. Never disturbed my nights, I assure you. Did they stop you sleeping?'

'No, not at all. Very comfortable night, kind of you to lend me the hut. But – well, it's somebody's holy place, even if it's not mine. I suppose it's just superstition, but I think we might get the parson to say the odd prayer. Would you be any happier, Bill?'

'Yes, I would, I think. Oh, not that I expect to sit up on the last day when the trumpet sounds minus the limbs that some future archaeologist has dug up from my grave. I'm being irrational, I know. But I'd just as soon leave the skeleton digging to someone else, you know.' Polly slipped her hand into his, and they sat together watching the shape of the ribcage emerge from the fine sand. The woman and two boys were working delicately with inch-wide paint brushes and blunt knives, pausing to blow the sand from the bones. Some of the other diggers had finished their tea and gathered around to watch, but Roger said,

'They're getting on fine. Ten more minutes, everybody, and then back to work, please.' He strolled off towards the beach.

'Gone to find a bush?' said Polly. 'What about you, Tamsin and Morwenna? I've got a potty in the car.' She went off holding the hands of her two daughters, and Thea sat contentedly with her back to the warm wood of the hut and one of her tiny black cigars in her hand.

'Lovely,' she said. 'So nice not to be digging.'

'You're not itching to get your hands on the site?' asked Randall Cooper.

'Not a bit, lovely just to rubberneck for a change,' she said not quite truthfully. He was looking at her with an interested, slightly quizzical stare. His face was the sort of large-boned, blue-eyed rectangle so common among Irishmen, so unlike the accepted version of the Celtic norm. From his voice he obviously had come, if long ago, from across that same sea which panted in their ears; perhaps the founder of the chapel which they were now disturbing had sailed on his millstone like St Brendan, or in his coracle, from those same shores.

'I've heard a lot about you, Professor Crawford,' he said in a lower voice. His large hand, faintly dappled with red hair, moved a little in the direction of hers. She thought, I know what he's heard. Either that I'm frightfully clever, and he's the sort of clever man happily married to a stupid woman who likes to think he'd have been happier with an intelligent one; or he's heard that Sylvester and I are living separately and thinks he only has to crook his finger and I'll come panting. Thea's life plan did not exclude amorous adventures. But they were to be on her own terms. She said, 'Really? From the Nankervises? I don't think I know anyone else who lives down here.'

'Oh, your reputation spreads wider than you think,' he said.

Thea did not answer, and sat watching the diggers and smoking. She could feel that Randall Cooper was watching her. She wondered how he would see her. She had heavy lidded grey eyes and a pointed profile; her dark hair was tied back in a bunch, which Sylvester said was unsuitable for anyone over the age of twenty-five. That was partly why she did it, of course.

The full form of the skeleton was emerging quickly and Thea was impressed at how much easier digging seemed to be on this light sandy soil. Already one could see the arch of the ribcage, and the long bones of the forearms above it in what must once have been a prayerful pose. The soil had not eaten away even the tiny bones of the fingers and knuckles though below the ribs the shape of a rabbit hole was revealed in section above the sacrum.

At six o'clock, the daily workers stood painfully upright, the older women rubbing their backs and arching their shoulders, the girls flexing blistered hands. Some of them gathered around the bones; the full length of the body was revealed now, from toes to skull. There were a few rotting teeth in the yellow jaw, and one of the girls remarked with a slightly hysterical giggle that he must have died from toothache. An older woman pointed out an arthritic swelling of the elbow joints, and Bill Nankervis, as he aimed a camera, thanked God for the twentieth century and aspirin.

Most of the workers collected up their belongings and trudged off towards cars, baths and rest, but several stayed to watch the exhumation. Mrs Dovey was working indefatigably, and though the two boys had taken several breaks they kept coming back to work with what Thea thought was commendable industry. She was unmoved by the fact that the remains were human, but had to admit that they held a powerful emotional appeal for most people. Roger Thurstan assured the workers that they had done marvels for one day and that a tarpaulin would protect what they had uncovered until they came back to get on with the work the next day, but all the diggers who were still there wanted to see the complete skeleton before leaving. In fact, if Thea had been in charge, she would not have permitted the work to continue, for one needed full daylight to appreciate the variations in soil colour from which the sequence of events could later be deduced, and Bill's photographs of the bones at every stage of disinterment would not be much more informative since he was taking them without a flash.

The sun had set in a picture postcard collection of colours by the time the remains lay revealed. The skeleton was almost complete and could have hung articulated in an anatomical laboratory. It was that of a tall man, Roger said, from his examination of the long bones and the narrowness of the pubic symphysis. Again Thea refrained from comment, but she would have sexed a skeleton, had she thought to try, from the frontal development of the skull and the thickness of the processes above the earhole. In fact the accepted practice, she would have thought, would be to wait upon the report of the osteologist.

The body had been placed in a hollow dug into the floor of the presumed chapel, lined with smallish chunks of the local slate on the bottom and sides. There must once have been a slab, perhaps inscribed, above it also, but the section, disturbed as it was by rabbit burrowing, seemed to show that there was a later trampled earth floor well above the level of the inhumation. The bones were well preserved and quickly drying in their exposure to the air. The ribs were already fading from their sodden ochre to an off-white shade. Mrs Dovey was giving a few valedictory strokes with her paintbrush to the cranium, Roger Thurstan was shaking out a sheet of polythene with which to protect the trench overnight, when Clovis shouted,

'Oh look, this isn't a vertebra. Look, sir, look, Mum, there's something here. Lying on the chap's ribcage. Can I pick it up, sir?' They gathered round to look where Clovis's finger pointed to a sand-encrusted, rectangular lump lying above the lower part of the spine. Again Thea itched to interfere. It was almost dark now, with the lingering west country dusk, and without floodlights nobody could see exactly what to do. The object should not even have been touched before it was photographed *in situ* and this applied particularly to something which was clearly extraneous to the skeleton, though it had been improper enough to continue with the disinterment of the bones even with inadequate light and recording. But bones at least were predictable. Bill said,

'I can't really take much of a picture of that now, old man. I can hardly see it myself in this light.' But Roger knelt gingerly down, and lifted the object out of the trench. They all watched as he brushed and blew the clinging sand from its surface. He murmured,

'It's quite hard, anyway. A bit of metal perhaps.' Little lumps and crumbs of wet sand fell away, and a shape emerged. He exclaimed,

'My God, it's a cross,' but in spite of his obvious excitement his hands were steady as he stroked away the grains of soil. At last he squatted back on his haunches, holding out the object for them all to see. Randall Cooper said,

'You've hit the jack-pot, old boy.' Thea held out her hand, and he placed the small object on her palm. It was a crucifix made out of some hard yellowish substance. She murmured, 'Might be whalebone, I suppose,' touching it with the tip of her little finger.

Clovis shouted, 'It looks like ivory,' but James Cooper said in an awed voice,

'But look at the carving, look at that. It's got creatures on it.' There was sand still clinging in the little crevices, but the boy was right. The crucifix was elaborately decorated with carved creatures, winged and stylised. The whole thing was about four inches long, and Thea could feel that its back, lying on her hand, was smooth. She said,

'Are you equipped to deal with this? It needs a good technician.'

Roger answered, 'You're right there. James, run to the hut and get the largest box with a lid you can find. That empty cigar box would be just the job.' He said to Thea, 'Put it back in wet sand for the time being, wouldn't you think? That seems to have preserved it for several hundred years.' He put a layer of damp sand at the bottom of the box which James had found, laid the cross on it, and sprinkled some more over until it was completely covered.

Randall Cooper said, 'Where will you put it for the night, old boy? Looks pretty valuable to me. Might even be treasure trove. Want me to lock it in the office safe?'

'Is it treasure trove?' Roger said to Bill. 'It never occurred to me. But I suppose Randall could be right.'

'I don't think so,' Bill answered. 'It's a branch of the law I'm rusty on, but I'd have thought only precious metals would be that. I could ring the local coroner and ask.' Thea interrupted,

'No need, it's not; only gold and silver and other such precious things are treasure trove. I don't know what this is made of but it's certainly not that. But Mr Cooper's right about its value. If this is a carved crucifix, provenanced exactly and datable from its context it must be worth thousands.' She could not resist adding, 'It's the greatest pity that Bill couldn't photograph it *in situ* before you took it out.'

'Couldn't we just put it back tomorrow?' one of the little boys asked. Thea waited until it was clear that Roger Thurstan was not going to answer himself, and then she said, the coldness in her voice aimed at him, 'That wouldn't be the same thing at all. But I would advise you to mark the exact spot.'

'It's getting almost too dark,' Roger said. But he put a small stone in the trench and then shook out the polythene sheet to cover it all, getting stones from the dump to hold it down at the edges. 'It should all be safe enough. After all, nobody knows we've found anything.'

'Aren't you staying here, then?' Randall Cooper said.

'No, I promised Celia I'd get back.'

Polly Nankervis had gone home some time before with her daughters and Thea and Clovis drove back to Buriton with Bill. She was glad to have an opportunity of getting to know her friend's husband, but her professional conscience was so much exercised by events at Pentowan that she could hardly think of anything else. Bill seemed to have realised that an exciting find had been made, but his digging experience, mostly with Roger Thurstan, had not been such as to make him aware of how disgracefully inadequate the excavation of that find had been. Thea was ashamed that she had sat by and watched the virtual plundering of an important site, but she still could not think what else she could at the time have done, even now with the benefit of hindsight showing her that there was more for an incompetent excavator to despoil than one skeleton.

Thea's own special subject was the prehistoric archaeology of Northern Europe, but she was sufficiently well up in other branches of her profession to be aware that Roger's find was of more than ordinary importance. Would he take proper care of it? Would he make sure that an expert in the conservation of small finds got immediate access to it? Was he even capable of continuing the excavation of what was obviously a very important site? What could Thea do – what had she authority to do? She sat and worried along these lines all the way back to Buriton.

VII

Thea found herself pining for the support of some senior colleague's advice. She simply did not know whether she had the right or the authority to interfere on Roger Thurstan's site, nor whether she was morally obliged to do so. The tools he was using belonged to the university and were presumably now hers to control: the land seemed to belong, unless Miss Ferris claimed it, to Randall Cooper, and apparently there were no other financial subventions for the enterprise, since the workers were volunteers and there was no question even of providing food for them as they came by the day. If the site were a scheduled ancient monument she would be able to get hold of one of her archaeological friends in the Department of the Environment to check what was going on, though it would be an invidious way of starting her career of collaboration with Roger Thurstan. But she could not find out whether the site was scheduled until Monday when the local council offices would be open.

Apart from the practical difficulties of stepping in to control what Roger was doing, Thea felt herself very much inhibited by the awkwardness of her personal position. Somehow it would be necessary to establish a working relationship with the young man, and he had already displayed his hostility. It would hardly be getting off on the right foot if she were to accuse him of professional incompetence, and, in effect, take his site away from him – especially a site where he had struck so lucky.

She thought of ringing up her own former boss, one of the professors at her college in London, or of asking advice from the by now very eminent archaeologist who had taught her as an undergraduate. But how to go about – the only word for it was sneaking – on her own new colleague? She had a perhaps unnecessarily defensive feeling about being both young and female as a Professor and Head of Department. When she had told Sylvester about her plans his polite and indulgent welcome for the news made it clearer than words could that he did not really think her capable of holding down such a position effectively. The implication had been that when his Far Eastern stunt was over she would be only too pleased to use his return as an excuse for leaving Buriton. She would not, could not give him the satisfaction of knowing that he had been right – though she realised that this was an unworthy thought and that Sylvester was more generous both than she gave him credit for and than most men would be.

The difficulty was multiplied by a complication which was not an archaeological one. There had been little opportunity to examine the crucifix, and Thea did not know what the carvings represented nor what the whole thing was made of; but no matter what the details of it were, the mania of rich men who thought it prudent to invest their money in durable objects had inflated the value of any collector's piece, whether its history was detailed from the day of its manufacture or whether it had appeared unprovenanced in a Levantine pawnshop. Some of Thea's colleagues made money on the side by pronouncing whether such things were genuine or forged. Now here was a piece which would probably fetch a high sale-room price for its own sake: in this case, when it had apparently been part of the burial clothes of a pious man whose remains had never since been moved, when it might even be attributable to a named owner (for there were presumably early records of religious sites in this part of the world and of the saintly people whom they commemorated), it would be almost priceless.

Thea walked restlessly up and down her small sitting-room. Unfortunately her own books had not yet arrived from London, except for the few she had brought with her that would be needed at the very beginning of term. She had nothing in which to look up parallels here. The university library was not open now and Clovis, asleep in his bunk next door, could not in any case be left alone. She went to the telephone, but there was no answer from the Thurstans' house; they must have gone out with the baby, who was still small enough to sleep in a portable cot. But she did not know quite what she would have said to Roger if he had been there.

Her uncomfortable meditations were interrupted by the telephone; it was Polly Nankervis. 'Thea, listen,' she said quickly. 'We completely forgot about that girl. So—'

'What girl?'

'Oh, Thea – the one who was looking for Miss Ferris. Julie Robertson.'

'Oh yes, I had forgotten her. But I'm sure it doesn't matter. She said she was staying near by with her family.'

'Well, I was worried about her, waiting all alone at that creepy house. And I thought she really might have found Miss Ferris, ill, or worse. So I went back after supper. And she was still there.'

'Silly ninny. What on earth was she up to? Had Miss Thingummy turned up?' asked Thea, not much interested in what seemed, for that day, a peripheral problem.

'No sign of Miss Ferris, no. Bill's quite worried about it, and he says he'll have to do something if she isn't there tomorrow. No, but I feel a bit guilty because we left the house unlocked, and we might have known the girl would go in again. Actually, you'll never guess what I found. She and her boy-friend have moved in, no less.'

'Moved in? What boy-friend?'

'Well, I had to do quite a bit of probing. I even had to say that my husband would get them prosecuted for house-breaking or something. It seems that she's not here with her family at all, but that she and her boy-friend came down on the boy's motor-bike, intending just to bum around St Ives with the layabouts there. You know, they sleep in bus shelters and live on milk they have stolen from doorsteps. Well, of course the prospect of a nice empty house with real beds was too much for them. In fact they were in, or on, one of the beds when I got there. What does baffle me, I must admit, is why they wanted to see the girl's old teacher at all. You'd have thought they would have kept well away.'

'No, I can understand that bit of it,' Thea said.

'Why, for goodness' sake?'

'Well, I should think that the girl wanted to flaunt her sexual relationship where it would hurt most. Apparently her family don't mind all that much, or she would hardly have told us exactly who she is, in case there were police out looking for her. She can't be more than sixteen at the outside. No, I guess she knew that Miss Ferris really would mind and couldn't resist it. Grinding her own past in the dirt, as it were.'

'You may well be right. Nasty little beast. Anyway, the thing is that she and Sid are still there and Miss Ferris isn't, so if you see them when you go over to the dig tomorrow you might point them out to Bill. He said they might as well sleep there tonight because she was so insistent that dear Miss Ferris would have invited them, but he's going over first thing to turn them out and check that nothing is missing that he knows of, and if Miss Ferris is still not back he says he'll have to tell the police.'

'That's all right then, out of your hands,' Thea said, without much interest. 'Did Bill tell you about the find at the dig?'

'Of course. He was frightfully bucked. But I expect you all were. Is it really something very special?'

'It's hard to tell in its present state. It'll have to be looked at by someone properly qualified. But I should think it does count as a quite important find for a site like this.'

'Won't Celia Thurstan be cock-a-hoop! I suppose it will get Roger on telly and all that, won't it? Think of the publicity.'

'I sincerely hope he's kept his mouth shut about it all,' Thea said energetically. 'For God's sake tell Bill not to utter until the thing's safely in some laboratory in London. Seriously, Polly, you know what people are like nowadays. The crucifix is well worth stealing, and the whole site could be rifled in a few hours if word gets round that there was anything special there. I tried to ring Roger Thurstan tonight actually, but there was no answer. I just hope he has the sense to keep his mouth shut, wherever he is.'

'Even if he has, you can be sure Celia won't.'

Polly might well have been right about Celia Thurstan.

Thea went early the next day, which was Sunday, to Pentowan, since she was anxious to impress his duties upon Roger: and found a scene of chaos, almost of devastation.

Roger Thurstan was standing literally wringing his hands when Thea came over the top of the sand dune. The polythene sheet above the skeleton had been thrown away, and was blowing in the wind, caught on some sea holly outside the beach hut. The bones of the skeleton were scattered, as though a dog had been scratching there, though it was obviously not a dog which had destroyed the grave, for the extent of the damage was such that one person would have had to be at work for much of the night. Not only was the first skeleton's grave now a deep and shapeless hole in the ground, but other meaningless pits had been hastily and carelessly dug all over the site. The dump was piled high and spilling over with sand and stones. The slate slabs which lined the first grave were flung at angles around it, and there were more, some lying on the ground, a few still wedged where they had been for a thousand years, with human bones in total disarray all over the site. There must have been at least five or six graves wantonly destroyed in the night. In a couple of places the stone wall, which had been visible yesterday only as a shadowed hump in the turf, was exposed, and the stones had been tugged at and were now tumbling from their positions. It was like a piece of Oxbridge College turf on which an army of moles had been let loose. What yesterday had been the neat remains of a chapel waiting for the excavator's trowel to expose their shape from the shroud of soil was now like a bombed site.

Thea, when she dug herself, felt about her sites as a sculptor might about an untouched block of stone, as though its true and meaningful shape were waiting for her to carve and reveal. What she saw before her now was like a blasphemy.

She walked slowly down towards Roger Thurstan. He was always pale, but he looked at her with a wild and exhausted face, and waved his arms in the air.

'My God,' he said. 'Will you look at this! It's ruined – totally ruined. Some madman – maniac's work. How could anyone —'

'I hope it isn't totally irretrievable,' Thea said calmly. It was obviously her duty to provide moral support. 'It ought still to be possible to get some sort of a sequence, though not what you might have hoped. It will be pretty tricky.'

'But the inhumation – look at it, bones scattered like autumn leaves. I – I'm in despair.'

'I don't blame you, I would be too. Have you any idea who might have done this? Who knew about yesterday's find?'

'Well, the local people have always known there were graves here.'

'No, I don't mean that. It seems pretty clear to me that there was some point to this – they were looking for something. It must be someone who heard you had found a "treasure" and came looking for more. Did you tell anyone? Where is the crucifix, anyway?'

'It's safe enough, at home. But who knew about it? I couldn't say. We were at a party last night, I should think the whole of Cornwall would know by now. I was rung up by a couple of papers and the BBC before I came out this morning.' Even now, Thea recognised a certain complacency in his voice as he said that. The crucifix would bring more than archaeological knowledge to this young man.

'But – would you think anyone found anything here? You don't think there might have been more? I can't bear the idea.'

'You were really rash to let anyone know about it. Don't you know the dangers of laymen treasure hunting on your sites? Really, I'm very sorry for you, it's dreadful to see an important site in this state. But I must tell you that I think you are very much to blame. It's been well known by practising archaeologists for some years now that treasure hunters will come and rifle any site that seems worth their trouble. Haven't you read all those circulars about electronic metal detectors and so on, put out by the Council for British Archaeology?'

'Really, Professor – no, I haven't. On my salary it isn't possible to subscribe to all the journals that people like you can afford, it's not to be expected for a family man. I really don't see how I could have known.'

'Well, I don't want to start recriminations, or to be disagreeable. This site isn't my responsibility, after all. But I am a relatively senior archaeologist now, not to mention the fact that I am your professor, and I think that I must say, with nobody else listening, that you have been lax in this matter. To excavate without keeping up with digging technique is as improper as to do so without keeping up with the subject itself, which I like to think you in fact do. And discretion about one's sites should be absolutely ingrained by now. I can't understand why you haven't read about the looting of other sites by treasure hunters. It's been going on for years. And especially as there is Randall Cooper's beach hut here – you could easily have slept here yourself to keep a guard. I just hope that you have put the crucifix somewhere safe until tomorrow. Then it should go straight to the Conservation Laboratories in London. And I think it will have to be taken in person now – obviously too many people know of its existence for it to be safe any other way.'

A slow, painful stain of red had spread over Roger Thurstan's face, and he did not answer for a moment. Thea was waiting for angry recriminations and wondering coldly how to cope with it. Verbal quarrels and insults were something which she had never encountered in adult life. In the end he said,

'Perhaps you're right, I was a bit careless. But you don't know what it's like for a married man. I – I'll swallow my pride, Professor, and ask you – what do you think I should do now?'

'The first thing is to get a bit of tidying up done here. There is no point in getting the police, as it's unfortunately not a criminal offence to trespass on land, and we have no evidence that there was any theft. You will have to dig at least one proper trench to get a sequence. And then if you think it's worth while you could strip the site down. It ought still to be possible to get some idea of how many graves there were and how they were arranged. And you can get a plan of the chapel, I suppose you have some diggers coming today?'

'Yes, some men too as it's Sunday. Not just my usual army of women.'

'Good, well you can make a start. And then it's absolutely essential to get that crucifix into a safe place. The Conservation Laboratory in London, I should think. It should be in a bottle of spirit now, you know, not in that sand, and above all it ought not to be lying round your house where anyone could get it. Could you take it up on the night train, perhaps?'

'Oh Lord – no, that's not on I'm afraid. I'm committed to appearing on Westward Television tomorrow, and to do a talk for the BBC from Plymouth. I said I'd have the object to display too.'

'You simply can't do that.'

'I did promise.'

'Yes well, I'm sorry that we seem to be starting our work together with dissension. But it's my clear duty to see that you look after that crucifix. I'll have to talk to its owner if you can't be made to see sense.'

'Really – you are taking a lot upon yourself,' he muttered resentfully. 'Why should I do what you say? It's my site.

And what do you mean by the crucifix's owner?'

'The landowner, of course. Randall Cooper, as far as I know. I'm sure he'll be reasonable at least. The thing means quite a lot of money to him, if he can substantiate his claim.'

'Do I hear my name being taken in vain?' a voice boomed above them. The large figure of Randall Cooper came slithering down the sand towards them. 'My word, what's been going on here? Couldn't you bear to wait, Roger? Or what?'

Roger Thurstan explained again what had happened as Randall Cooper wandered around the site, poking his conker-polished shoe at the various protrusions in the ground. Roger finished what he was saying like a small boy appealing over his mother's head to his father's higher authority: 'And now Professor Crawford wants me to leave all this – television and broadcast and all – and take the thing up to London tonight. You must see that I can't.'

'It's pretty valuable, is it?' Cooper said to Thea.

'Yes, I think it must be, though I haven't been able to look up comparative prices yet. But quite apart from its financial value, it must be preserved. A thing like that from a provenanced position is an absolute treasure when it comes to archaeological and historical information. It needs proper treatment by somebody highly skilled.'

'I suppose you're right. What about it, Roger old man?'

'Damn it all, I found the thing,' he said sulkily. 'You're treating me like a child.'

'If we're being accurate, it was found by my son,' Thea said coldly. 'In any case, we have no law of Finder's Keeper's in these circumstances. It belongs to the landowner, Randall here, or Rose Ferris.'

'No, no, it's mine all right,' Randall said quickly, and Roger said,

'OK, so it belongs to Randall. Jolly lucky for me actually. Do you remember saying that I could have fifty-fifty in any treasure we found?'

'That was a joke,' the big man said.

'Yes, I thought so at the time too. That party at the Vice-Chancellor's wasn't it? I must say I never thought to find anything worth a penny. Still, I'll hold you to it, old man. There were enough witnesses.'

Randall Cooper's highly coloured face seemed almost overripe as he looked at the pale young man. Then, with a visible effort he said, 'No point in talking about that at this stage. Have to find out what the thing is worth before it's worth discussing. But I agree with the professor. It should be got up to London pronto. I can take it if you won't, Roger.'

'Suppose I take it up?' said Thea. 'I know all the people at the Conservation Labs., I'll get it done straight away. And I wouldn't mind a day in Town.'

'If you want to,' Roger said ungraciously. 'I suppose I can't refuse. Though I don't know what I'll say to them at the television studios.'

'Get Bill Nankervis to develop one of his photographs,' Thea said unfeelingly, well aware that none of the film was likely to come out, taking in dusk as it had been. She felt revolted by the whole conversation. It made her realise that the unworldly ivory tower of a university was indeed her spiritual home, that she was able to attach so little importance to the monetary value of a find, and that she had so little sympathy with Roger Thurstan's excitement at the thought of the publicity it would bring him. He gave her the impression that it was the only aspect of the affair which interested him, and he and Randall Cooper were both callously indifferent to Rose Ferris's unexplained absence. As for Thea, she thought, and hoped she was not deceiving herself, that she would far prefer to dig without spectacular finds and without the danger of having her precious site rifled. Still, she admonished herself, it was easy enough for her to talk, with Sylvester ready to provide a meal ticket if she couldn't do so, and with her own disillusioned experience of publicity machines after being married to him for years. How could she tell what different characteristics the responsibilities of a family and the nagging of a dissatisfied spouse would have produced?

Thea arranged with Roger that she would call at his house to collect the crucifix. He seemed dubious about Celia's reaction, and told Thea exactly where the cigar box had been hidden. 'I'm not sure whether she'll give it to you,' he said dubiously. 'I'll write her a note.'

'I'll take proof of identity,' Thea said in a dry voice. Could Celia Thurstan possibly like knowing that her husband was afraid of her? In fact, if the woman was really such an ogre, she'd better get Polly Nankervis's company to collect the box. But the whole situation was absurd. Thea was looking forward to the opportunity, in London, of asking advice about how to treat Roger Thurstan. What a pity that she could not ask what to do about his wife. But that was the sort of problem which she should be able to deal with herself. It's a pity I need to meet the woman at all, she thought. Though it would have had to happen some time, in a small town like this. What a bore that people could be so difficult about personal relationships. Even if Sylvester were not a worldly success, even if she were not one in her own right, Thea could not imagine being as uncivilised in her behaviour as Celia apparently was. An education in small town life, Thea thought, and immediately reminded herself that one could find hundreds like Celia in London, it was just that she had never had to deal with one. It was the penalty of becoming a boss: the subordinates' families then affected one's life just as in-laws affected one's marriage.

Thea was surprised after all this to be greeted politely by Celia Thurstan. Polly had come along to provide protection, and as Celia went out to the kitchen to fetch the coffee which she had pressed on them, Thea whispered, 'The smile on the face of the tiger?'

They were sitting in the front room of the house, which was decorated in a style very familiar to Thea. It seemed to epitomise the tastes and ambitions of every young, ambitious, educated couple though one could detect a time-lag in fashion changes between London and places three hundred miles away. These particular objects and colours were perhaps a little passé. The room was badly kept and could have done with both tidying and cleaning. There was nappy fluff on all the upholstery, and half-chewed rusks and dampish clothes scattered around. Somebody had spilt a bottle of green ink over the books and papers on the glass coffee table, and it had dripped on to the straw carpeting and the baby was kicking on the floor, wearing a dashing but stained garment in purple stretch towelling.

Thea was pleased to find herself so little broody at the sight of him. For years she had been obliged to avert her eyes from babies, she had been so miserable about not being able to provide a sibling for Clovis. But this sallow little object, unbecomingly clothed and sour smelling, aroused no jealous feelings in her, and apparently few maternal feelings in his mother, for when she had put the tray on to a pile of old Sunday newspapers on the low table, she scooped him up and dumped him in a pram outside the window without a single affectionate glance or murmur. And yet, Thea thought, this was the apple of his father's eye.

Celia was wearing tight jeans and a shirt decorated with the portrait of a folk hero; the clothes were ill suited to her role. But she appeared friendly enough, and poured excellent coffee. Her smallish eyes darted from face to face, and she smiled and smiled, chattering and gesturing, telling Thea about her own education at one of America's most exclusive women's colleges, about Buriton's climate, about how much better they did this, that and the other in the States. Thea was no chauvinist, but it grated, and Polly looked as though she were itching to say, 'If you don't like it here, why don't you go back where you came from?'

'Still, it's getting more like home all the time,' Celia said. 'Credit cards, and out-of-town shopping, and all that. Not that we have that down here unfortunately.'

'It's no loss,' Polly said sharply. 'We still think human values are more important than profit margins I'm glad to say. I've never seen anything so horrible as one of those out-of-town shopping centres I saw in the Midlands when I went to stay with my sister. It was like 1984, loudspeakers haranguing you all the time, saying "Shoppers, hurry to so-and-so counter and buy your bargains quickly", and quantities of cheap and shoddy goods. Give me the corner shops in Buriton any time, where they know your name and give personal service.'

'That would be OK if you could get what you wanted, though it does waste time,' Celia said. 'But take yesterday, for instance, we went to a barbecue party and our hostess had to send to London for the charcoal.'

Thea said in a mollifying voice, 'Well, that's another of your transatlantic customs. Wasn't it a bit cold though, so late in the season?'

'Yuh, it always is too cold in this part of the world. But

the men enjoy it. Pretending they do the cooking. They never think of who has to clean it all up afterwards.'

'Oh, does Roger go in for barbecuing his own steaks?' said Polly.

'No. He'd rather starve than cook for himself. Even last night, at the Hendersons', he took off when the work started. Not that he'd be missed. What about you, Professor Crawford, does your husband help in the house?' This was said with a sidelong glance of those beady eyes which made Thea wonder whether the remark had an ulterior motive. Was Celia trying to embarrass Thea into admitting that the famous Sylvester Crawford had walked out on her?

'Yes, he does if it's necessary,' she said calmly. 'Though in fact we nearly always had an *au pair* girl. But do call me Thea, won't you? You make me feel so old.'

'Well—' Celia did not finish the sentence, but the implication was that Thea must be years older than Celia. Thea wondered whether open rudeness would not after all have been easier to cope with.

'If I'm to catch the night train I'd better get on,' she said. 'Shall I take that cigar box?'

'Yeah, sure – If I can find it. Now where did I put it last?'

'You haven't been handling the crucifix, have you?'

'Only to show to one or two people. There's been a lot of talk about it. Some people came back with me after the Hendersons' party to have a look.'

'It really shouldn't have been touched. Didn't Roger stop them?'

'He wasn't there. He had to go night-driving for the baby.'

'What do you mean?' Polly asked.

'Oh, he had to leave the party early because Henry kept

crying. He's done that every night, since he was born. I'd just leave him, let him exercise his lungs. But Roger got used to driving him around with the car-bed in the back of the car to make him shut up. He says it's easier than rocking him or pushing his carriage.'

'I knew someone else who had to do that,' Polly said sympathetically. 'Her baby used to cry till it was blue in the face, and sometimes even became unconscious. They used to drive round the streets of London in the middle of the night, and it started to wail every time the traffic lights were red. But surely your Henry should have grown out of the crying stage by now? How old is he?'

'Of course he should. He's eight months old. But he knows he's got his father just there, and I can't stop Roger spoiling him. Anyway, it keeps them both out of my hair,' Celia said, shaking her rather tangled black hair out of her eyes. She had been rootling in the wall cupboard as she spoke, a bulge of greyish skin protruding between her shirt and the waist band of her jeans, and now she stepped triumphantly off the arm of the sofa, clutching the small box. 'Here you are. I knew I'd put it somewhere safe, only you know how it is when you do that, you can never remember where the safe place was. I'll just check it's OK.'

Before Thea could stop her she had grasped the little cross ungently and held it up. 'There you are. Not much to write home about, I'd have thought. But as you all seem to think it's so special I guess I'm wrong. Let's just hope we get some money out of it, right?

Thea, in silent reproof, repacked it, and walked ahead of the other two women down the path to Polly's car. Celia lingered on her doorstep, and addressed Polly in the sort of voice which is intended to carry to third parties, but which could claim the defence of being confidentially addressed to one hearer.

'He's thrilled to pieces, naturally,' she said. 'All that publicity. Really pathetic.'

'I should think you would be too,' said Polly.

'Oh, he'll fluff up his chance as usual I guess. Just like he did the job here. I've given up hoping he'll ever get anywhere.'

'That's a bit hard, Celia. He's not exactly a failure.'

'What – a plain lecturer in a crummy place like this with a woman brought in over his head? It's hardly what you'd call a howling success. And now he says that all the publicity and what not with this find will give him his start. He sees himself as a TV star now, pulling in fat fees and being invited on lecture tours in the States. Some hopes.'

'Well, why not? It might well happen.'

'Not to Roger Thurstan. No, he's a sinking ship all right. If I had a raft I'd jump on it.'

'What do you mean? Leave him? But what about Henry? And you can't just leave someone because he isn't a worldly success.'

'You just watch me do it if I ever get the chance. You wouldn't see me for dust.'

Polly's face was quite pink as she climbed into the driving seat and snapped her seat-belt shut. 'That woman makes me see red,' she exclaimed. 'Goodness knows I'm not one for Women's Lib, but honestly, if she wants to be rich and famous she should jolly well go out and do something instead of just thinking it's that poor man's job to provide her with the moon if she cries for it.'

'Does he mind?' Thea asked. 'I haven't seen them together.'

'No, it's rather pathetic, he seems to love her devotedly, and she says the vilest things to him, quite embarrassing to listen to sometimes, and he doesn't seem to notice at all. Anyway, he'd never dare quarrel with her because he'd be so afraid of losing contact with the baby. He's besotted about it. Rather touching, really.'

Polly dropped Thea at the College, and the first thing she did was to repack the crucifix in layers of wet cotton wool which she shrouded in polythene. Then she put the whole parcel in among underwear in her small suitcase. She wished she could chain the whole thing to her wrist like a bank messenger. It would be too galling if after all it was she who let the thing get lost or stolen. She was reluctant to leave it even while she went down to dinner in Hall, and eventually only did so after putting the case under the thick padding of the Scandinavian quilt on Clovis's bunk, and double locking the door of his bedroom and of the flat.

Not many of the women dons attended the evening meal on Sundays, and Thea found herself eating corned beef and beetroot beside a very elderly woman, retired from active teaching but still publishing regular scholarly articles on minor details of medieval domestic economy, who introduced herself as Helen Eliot. Thea had often heard of her, and knew her to be over eighty, but she behaved with the decision and competence of a much younger woman, and Thea was again reminded of her conviction that the one way for a woman to keep herself worthwhile as a person, and not be degraded into condescension-worthy old ladyhood, was to carry on working.

Miss Eliot had white, shining short hair, in startling contrast to her large black eyes and aquiline nose, and she spoke with crisp, academic precision. Thea felt positively awed before this example of what she hoped one day to be herself – old, but organised, unpitiable, undefeated.

'I was very glad that they gave you the Chair,' Miss Eliot

said. 'It seems extraordinary, fifty years on, that I should still be thinking that it's a boost for women, but unfortunately the world hasn't changed in that particular. I must say, we all thought it would, but so many women turned tail and ran for the hearth as though it and their careers were mutually exclusive. I've sometimes wondered whether it wasn't the fault of people like myself – my generation of teachers, I mean. Perhaps our pupils were afraid of becoming like us.'

'Surely not.'

'Well, it was more unusual than not for my contemporaries to have children as well as do their work you know, even though it was easier for us to get servants than it is for you nowadays. I think we made the next generation feel that it was one or the other. But you have both, I believe? Didn't I see you in the college garden with a small boy?'

'Yes, I have one son. And I think the pendulum has swung back again. Most of my friends work, you know, as well as having families, usually more than one, too. But in one particular I'm sure things haven't changed – one still seems to arouse resentment simply by being a woman.'

'You say that with feeling,' Miss Eliot said sharply, looking at Thea under her hooded eyelids. 'Are you thinking of anyone in particular?'

'Oh – not really. I just don't feel entirely welcome in my new department, but it may be hypersensitivity.'

'It's that Thurstan boy, I suppose. Too handsome for his own good, I always thought, and with a very unhelpful wife. Don't let yourself be worried by him. What's he been up to?'

'Nothing specific: just a veiled atmosphere, you know. But he's been doing rather exciting work. He's digging over on the north coast on an early chapel site – about the Conquest period, I should think – and he's actually made a rather spectacular find.'

'Indeed. What was it?'

'It's a small cross, made of bone or ivory, I think, decorated with carvings. Not an unknown type, but a very good example. I'm delivering the thing to the Conservation Labs myself tomorrow.'

'How interesting. What do the carvings depict – could you see?'

'Yes, it hasn't been treated with quite the care it deserves and the sand has been cleaned off to show that there is at least one human figure, a man in a cloak, or cowl, with a shepherd's crook, carrying a sheep, and some winged animals.'

'That is very remarkable,' Miss Eliot said slowly. 'I notice that you refrain from saying by whom the sand was cleaned off. You display commendable restraint, if I may say so. But your description reminds me of something; will you come to my rooms after dinner while I look it up? I don't want to waste your time, but I can at least offer you some good Madeira to wash down the college cook's idea of a suitable cold supper for a Sunday. And some better coffee than they serve us in the Common Room, what's more.'

'I should be most honoured,' Thea answered formally, meaning it. 'Though I'm afraid I have to catch the night train.'

'Plenty of time, as they make us eat at such an uncivilised hour on Sundays. Let us go up now.' They rose from the table, and Thea copied Miss Eliot's formal bow to the Principal and followed her off the dais and from the room.

Miss Eliot's room was in the older part of the college, and was piled high with so many nostalgic possessions that it would not have been surprising to be told that she had lived there since the place was built at the turn of the century. Every inch of the walls was covered with pictures, framed silhouettes of ringleted children side by side with a painted glass scene showing the death of Lord Nelson and a John Piper lithograph. There were water colours both inept and excellent, an enormous black and white print showing a rake's drunken progress through nineteenth-century London and over the mantelpiece an oil portrait which Thea could have sworn was a Raeburn. The mantelpiece was crammed with photographs, and Miss Eliot said, 'I have twenty-three godchildren.'

There were waist-high book-shelves all round the room, as well as a couple of tall revolving bookcases. Thea picked up one of the books which was lying with a soft rag on it, and admired the calf binding.

'I've been treating the leather ones,' Miss Eliot explained. 'It's very soothing, like cleaning silver. Not that I have any of that any more. Look, I use this leather dressing made to a recipe from the British Museum. Do let me know if you would like some.' She showed Thea a square tin of oily fluid. But Thea never acquired things which needed upkeep; her cutlery was stainless steel and her furniture lacquered or laminated, if possible. She went on admiring the objects of affection and memory which covered every flat surface, including wooden inlaid boxes, porcelain bowls and animals, some fans, an eskimo soapstone carving and a huge pottery bowl of pot pourri.

The furniture was good, cherished Victorian and Georgian mahogany, and the chairs and sofa and curtains were the sort of flowered chintz which would seem at home in a genteel but slightly poverty stricken country house. Even the smell fitted – the pot pourri, and some freesias stuck into the mouth of a china spaniel, and applewood burning in the grate. It was charming, and Thea said so.

'I've lived here for so long, you see,' Miss Eliot answered, as she poured Madeira from a cut-glass decanter into tiny, lustred glasses. 'One does tend to accumulate things. I know I should clear it up – I often feel sorry for my executors – but I decided to leave my work in order first and that's an unending task. There always seems to be just one more article to write.' Thea sat sipping silently, and looking around with great contentment. This seemed just the way that an old woman should be, self-sufficient and productive, agreeable and undemanding. How much better Clovis and his children would be able to bear his mother in future years if she lived like this, she thought, having a lively fear of becoming the same sort of mother-in-law that she had herself – chirpy, fashionable, bored and terrified by old age. Helen Eliot was pulling books and periodicals from her shelves, and leafing through some of them. She asked Thea to be patient, and it was not difficult in this pleasant room. Thea looked affectionately at her hostess and enjoyed the excellent drink. How sensibly dressed, too, she thought, in a longish tweed skirt and thick dark stockings matching a cashmere jersey. It so happened that the clothes, and the 'Granny' shoes that went with them were fashionable for the very young at the time too. Thea would have bet that Helen Eliot's clothes had gracefully changed with current fashions for years, and that she had looked equally suitable in them all.

'Ah, here we are at last. I'm so sorry, I haven't quite the memory I once could claim,' the old woman said, sitting down beside Thea. 'Look, it's in this note I made of something from the Plymouth City Library. It was destroyed during the war, so sad. I'd been working there during the nineteen-thirties, but I never got round to publishing anything. Here we are, it was from an Inventory in a Visitation Book, belonging to the Dean and Chapter of Exeter. Truro wasn't a Diocese before the nineteenth century, as I'm sure you know, my dear. This is the Inventory of the monastery of St Filoc, and the interesting thing in this case is that so many of the objects mentioned in the thirteenth century were mentioned again at the time of the dissolution of the monasteries. Now, one of the objects that appears both times from St Filoc is a small ivory decorated cross showing the good shepherd. There's a quite detailed description – you can read the Latin, I take it. Look,' and she handed over a card covered with her own precise writing. Thea read:

*'Item i crux ossea in qua depictus iesus chr. dominus noster sicut imaginula pastoris ovem perditam recipientis.'**

'I imagine that such an object would not have been unique,' Thea said.

'It's so difficult to say, now when the relics we have are few and far between. Have we few because there were never more, or have we merely a tiny proportion of what once existed? I have wondered all my life. But your find, or rather, young Mr Thurstan's find, seems to show that there were at least two similar crosses. They might even once have been a pair, coming from spots so close together. We don't know exactly where St Filoc was, you know, but it is thought to have been in that stretch of the north coast. I look forward very eagerly to seeing your cross, my dear. No no, don't think of unpacking it now, an old woman's curiosity is not to be weighed against the preservation of an

* 'Item: one ivory cross on which Jesus Christ our Lord is shown, in the guise of the shepherd receiving the lost sheep.'

object like that. But from your description, it sounds very like. I wonder whether there might be a photograph. Perhaps I will telephone Mr Thurstan tomorrow.'

'I wonder if it's conceivably the same object,' Thea said thoughtfully. 'I don't believe in coincidence in this field. Two identical crosses would be too much for me to swallow. If I hadn't seen it come out of the grave myself —'

'How fortunate it is that you did. An accurately provenanced find of the period – that's treasure indeed. Now, my dear, I don't want you to miss your train. I am so glad to have met you – it will be a pleasure to have you in the College. Goodnight, goodnight.'

VIII

Thea determinedly thought herself lucky to have got a sleeping berth at all, on a weekend in September. It took some appreciating when she found that she had to share her compartment with a woman who got in at Truro with a two-year-old child, and asked Thea to let her have the bottom bunk – upon which Thea had already laid her nightgown and book – lest the child should fall out in the night. The woman looked tired and dejected, not like somebody who had benefited from a sunshine holiday, and Thea felt she could not refuse. But that was the most she could force from herself. She must think I'm a right bitch, she thought, as she transferred her belongings to the upper bunk, and gave a small wan smile in answer to the other woman's story of how the child had once fallen from the end of the bunk and rolled underneath it, so that when his mother woke from heavy sleep at his wailing she thought for a nightmarish few moments that he had become disembodied or disappeared. Undiscouraged, the woman chatted softly to her child, but Thea had to admit that she was quick in putting it to sleep and lying down herself at the other end of the narrow bed. Nor did she complain when Thea kept her small light on for a while and read. The child murmured a little, but not for long, and Thea was more disturbed than the couple below her by the train's frequent stops throughout Cornwall. It was not so much being bothered by the child – which she wasn't – as knowing that it would be natural for the child to make a noise which prevented Thea from relaxing; as though she were subconsciously preparing righteous indignation.

The last berth left had been, of course, in a compartment over the wheels, and Thea lay braced under the rough sheet as the train rattled and swayed over every set of points. She had taken a barbiturate pill, but it only induced dozing reveries, beginning with the visions of crashes, familiar to her from every journey of her life since Clovis had been born. There had been one phase when she could not go by car at all, so certain was she that travelling would kill or maim her. Now the fears were reserved for the journeys when she had time to remember them, and no statistical reassurance comforted her. As the train tilted round the sharp inclines of the west country permanent way, she was surprised each time as it came vertical again. She pictured the column of sleeping citizens projected into bloody screaming darkness.

She forced her thoughts on to the day behind and the day ahead. But she had sucked the subject dry in her brain. Round and round revolved the same problems about Roger Thurstan and her own responsibilities, like a donkey treading a water wheel. She thought of her list of specific remedies for sleepless nights, painfully developed during insomniac periods. It was a great drawback, she had always thought, to have too literal a mind to find solace in fantasies of a more perfect life. So she would work out her next article in her head, only to forget the lucid phrases when confronted by the typewriter: she would plan the organisation of her next excavation, series of lectures or dinner party, but now such thoughts set her tossing yet more restlessly. She had arrived at Buriton with sheafs of timetables and syllabus changes, and no worries about implementing them. But Roger Thurstan's attitude made it plain that there would be battles all the way.

She turned on the light and read another chapter of *Northanger Abbey*, but for once even the amiable inanities of Catherine Morland failed to divert her. What, after all, was the heroine, but an earlier version of the scruffy and impudent first-year students with whom she would be faced in three weeks time? Thea pulled the second blanket off the shelf and wrapped herself up cocoon-style. The child and his mother below were breathing deeply and regularly. It seemed almost insulting.

Would her students turn out to be like that girl at Pentowan? If so, she could prophesy that they would giggle at her behind their hands, mimic her clipped, affected voice and despise her preoccupation with things of the mind. Had Helen Eliot felt just that when her handpicked students forsook the outside world for hearth and home? Did she regard it as a rejection of what she was herself? Surely it was only in this century that people feared their juniors? And now it was the small hours, time for hot flushes of embarrassment of her own past mistakes and *faux pas*. It was the sort of night when they all, no holds barred, returned to humiliate her, from the time when she was twelve and had wet her pants in front of a friend's glamorous elder brother, to the episode this year when she had served uneatable fish to some of Sylvester's visiting firemen. And what about her behaviour at school with that pathetic Miss Cullen? Who was she to hate the young now if they dished out the same to her? One wouldn't have blamed Miss Ferris, yesterday, if she had been hiding from the girl who had arrived to flaunt her progression from dependence and admiration to scorn and derision. Miss Ferris could not help being aware that she was despised if she only caught sight of the smile on that chit's sharp face. Plain she'd be, in another ten years, a suburban virago nagging at her Sid and her kids, but full with the desirability of youth now. Thea felt, with loathing, the slackening flesh on her own upper arms, the incipient sag of her breasts. Miss Ferris, poor old thing, had been well out of that encounter.

Yet, where had she been? Thea pictured again that empty unlocked house, stark and bleak amidst its encircling sand dunes. A miserable place to live, she thought, but Polly had said that Miss Ferris loved it and meant to stay there for the rest of her life. Was she escaping from a hostile world, perhaps as the original hermit whose sanctity had attracted later worshippers and chapel builders had done a hundred yards away, many hundreds of years before? Or had the atmosphere of Dickensian childish Christmases deceived her?

Rose Ferris, Pentowan House: perhaps it was merely the elegance of the address which had attracted her. It was the sort of thing that Miss Cullen, twenty years before, would have liked. Thea visualised it set out in red capital letters along the top of a post card, or in copperplate on a visiting card; if you lived in that sort of house you would be sure to have cards, though goodness knows, nowadays, what you would use them for.

Suddenly Thea, who had been drifting into comfort if not sleep, jerked awake. Of course, she knew she'd seen the name somewhere when Polly Nankervis first mentioned it. That journey down on the train last week, when she had been alone in a first-class compartment with another woman whom she had thought might be going like herself to Barbican College, then she had seen that name and address, swinging in leather-bound luggage labels from the slightly shabby suitcase in the rack opposite her. That must have been Rose Ferris then. How silly of her not to realise it before. She racked her memory to summon up a picture of the woman.

She remembered her suddenly in great detail, with a quirk of sympathy and fellow feeling. Poor woman, journeying into loneliness and disappointment – for what else could her arrival at that dismal house have brought her? She had been waiting at Buriton Station for someone to meet her, a neat, inelegant, quelling woman. What was it the Nankervises had said? She had been left the property by a mad old aunt, and hadn't been down there herself for years. Would she even know whether the site Randall Cooper claimed was really hers? What a pathetic picture it conjured up, Thea reflected. And why did she, lying snug in her bed, bolstered by the awareness of a devoted son and a loving, if distant husband, of a good name in the world and exciting years of work ahead, why did she feel that she owed something to that unknown, once seen stranger? Was it because of the curious intimacy one felt with someone whose house one had explored in her absence, so inexplicably unkempt when one remembered its owner's disciplined appearance. Was it obscure guilt for her own long past cruelty to Miss Cullen – did her subconscious wish to atone by making up for the spite she had recognised in Julie Robertson's sharp face? Oh God, she thought sleepily, not deep psychological inner meanings now ... I'll go and see the old thing when I get back, and probably get no thanks for it either ... She slept lightly, wheels churning in her slumber; and when she was next aware, the train had been at the Paddington platform for two hours.

It was disconcerting to arrive in London and not have her own house and bathroom to go to. Thea wondered whether to wish herself upon a friend for breakfast, but in the end she went into the station hotel and ate hugely to fill in the time, feeling like an alien. She held on to the suitcase all the time, and counted the minutes till she could hand its burden over. But her friends at the Conservation Laboratories would not arrive at work till getting on for ten in the morning. In London at this time, six months ago, Thea herself would have been rushing around her house to leave it looking like home before she went off for the day to the university. What else could one do in a London early morning? Eventually she went to her hairdresser, and astonished the youth by appearing so early and by holding her case on her lap throughout his treatment.

At last, at a civilised hour, she took a taxi to Bloomsbury, and was pleased and reassured by the warmth of her welcome. The Deputy Director of the laboratory had been with her on a conservation course in both their pre-undergraduate days, when she had been fired by an interest in the objects they learned to treat, and he by the methods of treatment. His name was Helmuth Muller; his father had been at the West German Embassy at that time, and Helmuth was merely supposed to be learning English in a more constructive and natural way than he would have done at language lessons. It had greatly annoyed his father that he had also learnt to love the English, and had decided to stay. Now, in spite of a slight accent, he dressed like a country squire and looked like a Professor. His wife was the daughter of an Irish peer, and his children were at Benenden.

'My dear girl, how delightful,' he said, kissing Thea neatly beside her mouth. 'We thought you'd disappeared to the wilds. Ginny was saying last night what a shame it is never to see you. Let me ring her up and she can meet us for lunch.'

Thea agreed, but insisted on business first, and was gratified by Helmuth's enthusiasm at the sight of the crucifix. She wondered whether she could take it for one of her former colleagues at the university to see, but Helmuth would not let it out of his hands untreated, and insisted on summoning a squad of apprentices and underlings to admire. However he had some photographs taken and instantly developed, and Thea was able to go to the university armed with a sheaf of them after a long and boozy lunch in Helmuth's latest 'find' of a restaurant.

Professor Vivian, to her disappointment, was still away. It was he from whom she had hoped for advice on her treatment of the difficult Roger Thurstan, and she could not bring herself to ask anyone else about that problem. He was the only one who, she was sure, would not at once tell all their colleagues that Thea had found the job too much for her before the first term ever began. But Dr Mayor was in, and free to help. His reaction to the photographs of the cross was all that Thea had expected from a specialist in the post-Roman period; he said that a find of that nature, dated by its context and professionally excavated was priceless. It was revealing that he pursed his lips when Thea told him the name of the excavations director; he did not, he said, know anyone of that name working in his field. Was Thea sure that he—? Yes? Well, there must be something wrong with a lecturer of several years standing who claimed to specialise in the pre-Conquest period, of whom Dr Mayor had not heard. But all departments carried the odd passenger, he added, sighing. He was a man, as all his colleagues knew, without humour and with an overgrown academic conscience, but his judgement was sound, and Thea felt confirmed in her own reservations about young Thurstan, though no nearer to knowing what to do about them.

She slept better during the second night on the train,

partly because she was alone and partly from exhaustion. She had done less in that one day than every day when she lived in London, but she already felt the country visitor's strangeness. And the cool, rain-washed, sea-scented streets of Buriton the next morning felt like home.

IX

Thea never breakfasted in hall, so that though she arrived in college before even the kitchen maids were out of bed she was able to make herself coffee and toast in her own flat. Afterwards, there seemed, as there had in London, to be a gaping period when she could not quite think what to do until it was time for the day to start. But Thea decided that this was a problem which she would have to solve at once and for ever; if she was to stay in West Cornwall there would be many early arrivals off night trains both here and in London. Today, she went out again to the beach, and strolled along the oily sand, admiring the picturesque sea front of Buriton seen from the shore, the glittering lighthouse and domed observatory, and admiring most of all her own energy in being there. It must be, she realised, five years since she had last gone for a walk; and before that the walks had not been voluntary but Clovis quieteners.

The day spread rather unenticingly ahead; she could go and be depressed by the mess at Pentowan, and at the same time make her amends to Miss Ferris, who would not realise that Thea's friendliness was self-induced, to ease her conscience. There was no doubt more work to do in the department, though her courage cringed at the thought of Miss Blake, who could hardly have been replaced yet. In the end, Thea returned to Barbican College to call on Helen Eliot with the photographs taken at the Conservation Laboratories.

By the time Thea got back to the college there was more

activity going on, though the place still seemed echoing and lonely with so few students in residence; Thea walked along the undecorated corridors hugging her shoulders in the 'College slouch' of her own undergraduate days. Barbican, like the other women's colleges with which Thea was familiar, had grown from one largish house into a conglomeration of buildings of various dates, joined to one another by these long tiled passages. She wondered why, now that students were so much less inhibited than in her own youth, none of them had cheered up the walls with a few murals, or even graffiti.

The outer door of Miss Eliot's rooms was closed, and there was no answer to Thea's knock. Thea waited for a moment till it would be polite to knock again more loudly. This was the oldest part of the college; the William Morris paper on the walls might even be an original one. There were pictures here, framed drawings and photographs of classical statues in limited stages of undress; and there were overflow shelves from the dons' own rooms of books which were not likely to be consulted again; one contained rows of detective novels.

The door opposite opened, bringing with it a wet bathroom smell of steam and soap and talcum powder. A youngish woman came out carrying a towel and a sponge bag, and smiled at Thea.

'Hullo! I know, you're the new professor. Thea Crawford, isn't it? I'm Anna Morgan. Philosophy. I saw you at dinner the other night but didn't have a chance to meet you. Is everything all right? One can feel awfully strange here – I know I did at first. All the others are so afraid of seeming to intrude. The only result with me was that I thought I must smell.'

'How do you do? No, I'm settling in very well, people

seem very kind. And they've given me a lovely flat.'

'I know – in the new block. But that's because you've got a little boy. More privacy but smaller rooms. You must come and have a look at mine. I've got acres, even if it does mean sharing a bathroom with old Helen.'

'Actually I was waiting to see her. But she seems to be out.'

'That's funny. Are you sure? One can usually set a clock by her. I thought it was a bit odd that I was first in the bathroom today. She usually gets up terribly early because old people don't need so much sleep, she says. In fact she makes tea in bed sometimes in the small hours and sits there writing to her numerous godchildren. She's a darling. Knock again – she must be up. And she can't have gone out without setting foot in the bathroom.' Thea rapped loudly at the white-panelled door, but there was still no reply. Anna Morgan frowned.

'I don't like that much,' she said. 'After all, she is over eighty. Look, hang on. I'm going to get the porter to come and open the door.'

'Do you think – is that necessary?'

'Oh, you needn't worry about Helen being cross. She never is. And we can't just leave it. I won't be long.' And she ran off, looking, with her long hair and tight jeans, more like a first-year student than a teacher of, good heavens, philosophy. Thea perched on a window sill overlooking the garden to wait for her to come back. The sun warmed her back, and there was an agreeable humming of a distant lawn mower. It was, she decided, very nice at Barbican College. And the management of the place was excellent. This passage was spotlessly clean, and smelt of lemon-scented floor polish, not of the usual institution disinfectant, mingled with Anna Morgan's bathroom cosmetics, and something else – what was it? Bonfires? Something vaguely singed, at least. There was probably an ironing room somewhere along here, unless places like this had automated laundries downstairs for the lucky students these days.

Anna Morgan came back followed by one of the porters. He carried a bunch of keys, and smiled at Thea.

'We'll just make sure the old lady is all right, miss,' he said paternally. 'Wouldn't like to think anything could have happened to Miss Eliot. Been here as long as I can remember, she has, and that's going back some way.' He tried a couple of keys, and the third one turned in the lock. The inner door was also closed, and he tapped on it, and then pushed it open. The smell of burning was much stronger here. The room was in darkness, and the porter called 'Miss Eliot? Are you in bed?' and when there was no answer, he went over to draw back the heavily lined curtains. Then the man groaned, Anna Morgan screamed, and Thea stood as though petrified.

Helen Eliot was lying on her own hearthrug, her skirt grotesquely hitched up to reveal long pink bloomers, one arm flung out, the other folded under her body. The singeing smell had come from the fire which was now burnt out to a pile of fine ashes. It had caught her white hair leaving it frizzled and browned at the ends. On the parquet surround of the flowered carpet was a pool of some oily fluid, and an overturned square tin, which Thea recognised as the leather dressing which Helen Eliot had shown her on Sunday. And when they crept closer, they could see that on her temple was a mottled ugly bruise.

The porter knelt down and felt the pulse, but he said, 'Icy cold. She must have been gone for hours, poor lady.' There were tears rolling down his grey cheeks, and he wiped them on the sleeve of his overall.

'We can't leave her like this,' Anna Morgan cried. 'Help me lift her on to the sofa at least.'

'It won't help her, my dear,' Thea said gently. 'As Pooley says, she must have died last night. Look, the fire is quite burnt out and cold. She must have slipped and fallen, and died without regaining consciousness. Anna, listen to me.' She took hold of the girl's shoulders and shook her gently. She was hardly more than a child herself, philosopher or no. 'Miss Eliot was very old, and she can hardly have suffered. She was working and in possession of her faculties right to the end. Wouldn't you choose to die suddenly without any illness or diminution in your powers?'

'But you can't – how do you know? Oh, I can't bear it, she must have been lying there all night, right next door to me, and I never knew, I never did anything to help. Oh, we must get a doctor at least.'

The porter said, 'That's right, I'll see to that. I know who her doctor was. And it'll mean the police and an inquest I'm afraid, for the poor lady. But you've no call to worry about that miss, you go and have a nice lay down and a cup of tea. You've had a shock. There's nothing you can do here now.'

Thea was extraordinarily distressed herself, considering how brief her acquaintance with Helen Eliot had been, and how ardently she felt, and told Clovis, that it was wrong to mourn the quick death of an old person; neither was Anna Morgan's academic philosophy any help to her, and Thea had almost to heave her back into her own room – huge, messy, postered and cushioned. In fact there were no chairs, and Thea pushed the girl down on to a leather floor sack, which moulded itself to her form as she lay and sobbed. Thea silently handed her a towel, since there were neither cloth nor paper handkerchiefs to be seen, and then, drawing on her memories of similar buildings, went along the corridor to find the small kitchen where students could boil kettles. There she found a tin of coffee and some sticky mugs, and brought back a distasteful but hot and sweet brew as medicine for shock.

'I'm sorry,' Anna gulped.

'That's all right,' Thea answered. She felt no rush of sympathy to the head now any more than she ever did, but she had often assured herself that intelligent actions were more useful than outpourings of heartfelt compassion, and the end result was intellectually indistinguishable. So now she sat down on Anna's unmade bed, and set herself to listen.

'I feel so awful,' Anna said unnecessarily. 'If only I had known, I should have heard. I could have saved her.'

'But, Anna, she must have been knocked unconscious on the corner of the fender at once. There wouldn't have been anything to hear, even if one could through these walls.'

'Oh yes yes, you can hear. She was so nice about my guitar and record player, I'm sure she must have hated it really but she always said she didn't, and she used to say it was an education for her to hear that sort of music, she said it was a great improvement on what they listened to when she was young. I used to hear her typing. And she had a visitor last night too, a man. I can always hear that through the walls, though not women unless they laugh. Funny, isn't it?'

'An odd acoustic fact.'

'And why did she have to slip last night? She had so much work to do – think of the people the world can spare. Oh, it isn't fair. What was she doing, anyway?'

'She must have slipped on that leather dressing that was spilt.'

'What was that? I didn't see anything except – her.'

'It was something she showed me when I was in there on Sunday evening. A polish for the leather bindings of her old books. The tin was on the mantelpiece, I remember, it must have fallen off and spilt, and she slipped in it. Terribly greasy stuff I should think.'

Anna Morgan continued in the same vein for some time, and it was nearly twelve before Thea felt she could leave the girl to dress and get herself organised; and by then Thea felt she had done more than her duty by her. One would have thought, she told herself severely on the way back to her own flat, that the intensive study of the teachings of the world's great minds on how to bear the human condition would provide some solace when it came to suffering in person one of its problems.

There were messages in her flat that Thea was to go and see the Principal of the college at her convenience, and from the porter to say that arrangements had been made with a local undertaker, and from a police sergeant to say that he would call that afternoon to take her routine statement, and a fourth to the effect that the inquest had already been booked for that Friday. There was nothing about the funeral service. But when Thea called on the Principal that afternoon, she was told that it was well known in the college that Helen Eliot had been an agnostic, and had frequently declared that she only wanted to be plonked unceremoniously in the soil somewhere.

Thea commented that people of that type usually stipulated cremation and the Principal smiled. 'No, no, you don't understand. Helen Eliot's father was a naturalist – one of Darwin's followers in actual fact – and he brought his family up to know all about fertilisation of the soil and nitrogen cycles and that sort of thing. You wouldn't think it from only meeting her recently, but Helen was a tremendous good-causer in her younger days, and one of her platforms was the anti-cremation one. She compared humanity to the earthworm, usually unfavourably. We're not so useful to the earth, it seems.'

'Was she a suffragist, in fact?'

'Yes indeed, but not a militant one. I'm sure she never raised even her voice in anger in her life. We'll have a concert in remembrance of her when the term starts. Something solemn but secular. It's a mercy she died so quickly, you know, because she would have hated being looked after.'

'Yes, I was trying to get that across to Anna Morgan, not very successfully I fear.'

'Oh dear, no you wouldn't. Poor Miss Morgan, she's one of our more emotional members. Tells all her students that the only use philosophers had was to show that the heart is worth more than the head. It makes them disagree you know, which is wonderfully salutary for the young. But I mustn't indulge myself with college gossip just now – have another cup of coffee, do help yourself – I really asked you to come because I want your advice about Helen Eliot's work. Our other historian is away this term, and I expect there's quite a lot which is in the press or nearly ready for publication. She was such a prolific writer, even these last few years. Now, can you help about this? I'm a scientist myself, don't know a thing about history. I know she left all her books and papers to the college, so we'll have to do something about it.'

'I could have a look, I suppose,' Thea said slowly. 'It's not that I don't want to – please don't think that – but it's years since I did any proper history. We think of archaeology as being almost a scientific discipline these days.'

'Oh dear, do you really? I knew you'd gone in for computers and expensive gadgets like that, but I must say I wouldn't have thought of it as a science.'

'We like to see it as an amalgam: the marriage of the two cultures, if one is being pompous. But I did read history for a while when I was an undergraduate. Suppose I have a look and see how much there is to do? It may just be a bit of proof correcting or typing. And if there's more at least I can find out who is the right person to deal with it.'

But Thea had routine duties too, and she arrived to a scene of fury and chaos when she went in to the department.

Roger Thurstan was stalking up and down the passage with his face set in a Byronic sneer, self-consciously shaking his hair back from his forehead in the intervals of running his fingers distractedly through it. 'There you are,' he said abruptly to Thea. 'I've been waiting for you. What's this about Helen Eliot popping off? I saw her myself yesterday. And now here's a new secretary, I don't know what's happened to Elizabeth Blake. And she won't let me get at the filing cabinet – I ask you. And Randall Cooper's rung you three times already about my crucifix. I'd have thought you might have let me know about it yourself. And there's police all over the place at Pentowan. That's why I am here. It really is too bad, I don't know how I'm expected to get any work done.'

The new secretary came out of her room, and it was clear that if she had been that sort of person she too would have been tearing her hair.

'Good morning, Professor Crawford,' she said quietly, not looking at Roger Thurstan. 'I am Mrs Tobias. I started work here yesterday, but I have been waiting for your instructions.' She emphasised the word 'your', flashing a slightly malicious glance at Roger. She was a dumpy woman of about fifty, tightly corseted and with rigidly permed hair. She could have worn a placard proclaiming that she was a stickler for every sort of propriety, and Thea wondered whether the Registrar had thought to serve her right for complaining about Miss Blake. But her first opinion was deceptive. Mrs Tobias quickly showed herself to be admirably efficient and impersonal: she had not refused the keys of the filing cabinet to Roger out of spite or personal animus against handsome young men but simply because her training had taught her that the head of the department was the only person with a right of access to them. In fact, as Thea was looking through the neatly sorted mail she heard the woman say to Roger that she would type his letters later in the day if there was time; but that she must naturally hold herself first at the Professor's disposal. Roger stumped into his own room and slammed the door, and a little later started an amateurish tapping at his own machine. Thea looked across at Mrs Tobias to see whether she would meet a glance of amused complicity at the waves of resentment projected through the partition wall, but the secretary was looking demurely at the pad on her knee, pencil poised. Thea, who had felt like a moment's relaxation after the chaos she had left behind in college, felt morally obliged to deal with all the tedious letters; she said to Mrs Tobias,

'Tell me, do you think there's going to be administrative work on this scale all the time, or is this just the beginning of the academic year? I'm quite new to this job, as you probably know.'

'It should slacken a little, Professor. I used to work for the professor of Greek, and things seemed to become easier as the year wore on. Though he would often complain that he had very little time for his own research.'

'I see. I hope you don't mind having been transferred?'

'Oh no, I asked the Registry to transfer me when my professor retired. I had worked for him so long, I did not think I should have enjoyed seeing another man sitting in his chair. I've been employed at the university for fifteen years, ever since my husband died.'

'That will be tremendous help to me,' Thea said. 'I'm completely strange here, you'll be able to tell me what to do.'

'I hope to be of service, naturally. I do hope there won't be difficulties,' she said, looking marginally less rigid. 'I've heard Miss Blake talking in the coffee room, one could hardly avoid it. So Mr Thurstan's attitude wasn't a complete surprise to me. I do hope he'll get over his disappointment.'

'I'm afraid I knew nothing of all this till I met him,' Thea said slowly, wondering whether it was a proper subject to mention now. 'But after all, it can't be very nice for him to have me put in over his head. One can see that he wouldn't like it.'

'He must learn to thole it,' Mrs Tobias said severely. 'My goodness, where should we all be if we gave in to every disappointment? He should show more dignity, a man in a responsible position like that. I was quite shocked. And he's not very polite, Professor. I may have to ask you to speak to him. He hasn't spoken to me as he ought, and he was being positively offensive to the gentleman who rang up to speak to you. I feel that you should know.'

'Well, thank you,' Thea said helplessly. 'We'll just ride it out if we can, I think. Now then, does Mr Cooper want to be rung back?' Mrs Tobias was standing up to dial the number when the telephone rang, and Thea caused manifest offence by automatically lifting the receiver herself. I must get used to being a secretary's boss, she thought, as she said, 'Department of Archaeology.' It was a personal call for Thea from the Conservation Laboratories in London, and she waved Mrs Tobias to go back to her own room and get on with the pile of mail. Helmuth Muller's voice came along the line more distorted by distance than it would from New York to London, and his accent, hardly perceptible face to face, sounded far more pronouncedly Teutonic.

'Thea, my love,' he said. 'Such a delight to see you yesterday, my poor exile.'

'No no,' she protested laughing. 'I'm perfectly happy.'

'Good, good. I thought you looked a little tired. But to business, I don't ring just to waste your time. The crucifix, Thea, that nice little cross. It's ivory, by the way, as you knew, a walrus tusk. Very nice, charming little thing, but it doesn't fit with what I thought you told me about it. I just wanted to ask you again about how it was found. I thought you said you saw it exhumed yourself from a definitely stratified grave, undisturbed.'

'Yes, that's what I said.'

'Well, my dear – don't think I doubt your competence, not for a moment. That just makes it all the more interesting.'

'Why, Helmuth? You sound dubious.'

'It's the impregnation, its state of preservation. Now, I admit that as far as I'm aware it's unique, I haven't anything to compare it with, no other ivory interred in sand for centuries that we know precisely of. But the analysis was most unexpected. Could they have burnt something like incense then? And would it have survived? I shall write an article about it. I hope you don't mind if we hang on to it a little longer than I said at first, it's one of the most intriguing problems I've come across for a long time – so grateful to you for bringing it my way.'

Thea felt, without at all knowing why, as embarrassed as though she had dropped a fearful clanger in public. She put her hand to her cheek and felt it flushing, though part of her mind was thinking that she had no reason to take this personally: it was no skin off her nose, she might say. She said, 'Well, Helmuth,' and thought how on the defensive sentences beginning like that made one sound, 'I didn't actually dig it up myself, but I was there. I'd have said the thing had been in the ground for getting on for a thousand years. The site's definitely about the period of the conquest, and the skeleton hadn't been disturbed.'

'Yes, yes, the skeleton, can you let me have that too? I'd like to get some tests done on it for comparison. We have a very good girl on bones here at the moment. You see, the thing is that we have traces of resin in the interstices of the design, and I needn't tell you that there's no recorded use of incense until much later. And it's not wet enough, I'd have said, should be saturated, though there again, it may be different on these sandy sites. Delightful, my dear. A treat for an old enthusiast like me.'

'How much longer would you want to keep it?'

'A few days, there are still several tests. You don't mind, I take it?'

'It's not mine, I told you, Helmuth. I'll talk to the owner about it though. I'm sure nobody could object to your hanging on to the thing for a while.' Helmuth Muller rang off after some flowery compliments and Thea sat for a moment suffused by undefined worries before ringing through on the inter-com to ask Roger to come into her room. He stalked in looking proud and martyred, and stood looking at the view, with an aura of conscious suffering. Thea told him what Helmuth Muller had said about the crucifix, and he burst out,

'For God's sake, as though there weren't enough trouble for one day. That's all I need – you'll be accusing me of conjuring tricks next I suppose.'

'How ridiculous you're being – it's nothing to do with me except that the chap at the conservation labs happens to be a friend of mine. 'I'm simply telling you what he said. I should have thought it made a fascinating archaeological problem.'

'Yes, I suppose you're right,' he muttered grudgingly. 'Sorry.'

'Well, I was wondering whether we might look together at Bill Nankervis's photographs since we haven't any hope of reconstructing the original stratification. I gather you called the police in about the vandalism, from what you said about them being all over the place at Pentowan. I'm surprised you managed to persuade them to show any interest.'

'I didn't, in fact didn't even ask them. It would have been useless. No, for some crazy reason Bill Nankervis sicked them on to the place, looking for the old woman from the big house.'

'No, did he really? I was worried about her too. Have they found her?'

'I don't know. It's of no interest to me. Never saw her. My aunt always said she was a dead loss, anyway.'

Thea looked a question, and he went on, 'My old aunt that worked for Miss Trevanion. Her maid, in fact. Surely they've told you that I'm a working-class boy?' Nothing irritated Thea more than such declarations, though they came more usually from her students than from colleagues, who had, on the whole, grown out of saying that sort of thing. She said, mildly,

'I never know what people mean by that nowadays. I'd have thought that your job and the way you live made you middle class by definition, whatever your family were, if it matters.'

'Oh, it matters all right. You don't know, it's obvious you haven't ever experienced the discrimination that comes the way of people like me. There's a conspiracy, not just against me, but against people like me, on the media, in universities, in professions. I have to be five times as good as anyone else to get where they do in this country. Like an American Negro, that's what Celia says.'

'Oh really, that's rubbish, Roger, and you must know it. Not to mention the fact that you're stealing my lines. All that's what women tend to say.'

'Yeah, well, it's not the same thing. Anyway, my family were working class, farm labourers and so on. And one of my aunts worked for old Victoria Trevanion at Pentowan until she died.'

'Oh, I see. Did you live in that part of the world yourself, then? Is that how you knew about the site?'

'My home was quite near, yes. Though my father's dead now. His life was too hard for him to live to a great age, being poor.'

'If you've still got a chip on your shoulder after all these years there isn't much point in my trying to knock it off. And honestly, I don't care if you want to treat me as a bloated capitalist. I just wish you could manage to keep it out of the office. I don't go round spouting about the liberation of women when other people are trying to talk about something like their own work. What I want to know is about the excavation of the crucifix. It presents a most odd problem, doesn't it. Do you think any of those photographs came out?'

It took quite a bit more coaxing to get Roger to discuss the matter sensibly. Thea wondered whether married life was like this for most women, did they have to produce prolonged persuasions of this nature before their husbands ended up wound round their little fingers? It made her profoundly grateful for Sylvester, if so, but even more apprehensive for the future of her departmental work. What an unspeakable bore it would be if she had to degrade herself by winning Roger over with feminine wiles every time she wanted anything done. It was beginning to look as though he were so stuck in his role as a downtrodden representative of the underprivileged that it would be impossible to reach any rational basis of co-operation with him. And staff in British universities were virtually unsackable, too, she thought gloomily. The only thing to do would be to write brilliant articles for him to publish under his name so that some other university could be deceived into appointing him to a higher position, and get him out of her hair. Or perhaps he could earn a better living by presenting that handsome profile.

'How did the telly appearance go?' she said idly.

'Oh, I'd have thought that was too small beer for you to know it existed. Regional, provincial, all that. But it went all right, I suppose. It was a nuisance not having the cross to display.'

'Any audience reaction?'

'I wouldn't know. But plenty of trouble locally. I told you when you came in, though I don't suppose you were listening. Randall Cooper wants the thing, he says it's his, though he promised me a half share in the value of anything we found and I don't suppose he can wriggle out of that, too many people heard him say it. What do you suppose it's worth?'

'A small fortune. I'm told that the last walrus ivory cross, which wasn't provenanced, fetched thousands several years ago from the V & A.'

'My God, couldn't I just use a bit of that,' he sighed. 'But now there's more trouble, that's why Cooper has been getting so agitated. Bill Nankervis has been making a nuisance of himself – the last person you'd have expected it of. He says the land isn't Randall's at all, that it really belongs to the Trevanion estate or something. I don't understand why, some pettifogging lawyer's detail. But if I'm diddled out of my share —'

Thea heard more about that in the evening, when she was visiting a rather embarrassed Polly, who did not seem sure whether it was disloyalty to discuss the matter. Bill apparently was caught between two stools, fires, duties or whatever. The facts, as appeared from a muddled and inexpert explanation from Polly, were that the site of the dig had originally been part of the Pentowan estate and belonged to the Trevanion family. Several years ago, Randall Cooper had erected his little hut, and fenced in a plot in the pit enclosed by the sand dunes and the cliffside, and had used it ever since as his weekend hide-out. When Miss Victoria Trevanion died, Randall Cooper had then approached Bill, who was the sole executor and in whom the property was now vested until payments of debts (there were none, except to the estate duty office) and distribution of assets; all was in fact left to Rose Ferris, in a will made just after the war.

Bill knew that most of the land would have to be sold to pay death duties in any case. He had really expected to sell the whole lot on the assumption that a London-based woman of no great age would much rather have cash than a gaunt and uncomfortable house in the middle of nowhere, and he had been very surprised when Rose Ferris had bombarded him with letters in her tiny script, abjuring him to dispose of no more than was absolutely unavoidable. He felt as he listed each acre, that he had been squeezing out drops of her blood, from the written squawks, Polly said.

As a matter of fact, Polly said, as though Thea were doubting it, Bill was the most scrupulous solicitor one would imagine, he absolutely exuded virtue and uprightness and all that. Anyone could see it. So he naturally had terrific qualms about selling the land at Pentowan privately to a friend of his, and he dithered for ages about whether it wasn't his duty to have auctions and advertisements and all that. He never thought that Randall would get planning permission to do a thing on it, and nor did anyone else. It was still a mystery how he had swung it, or whether he had known in advance that he wasn't gambling except on a certainty, and if so how. After all, that bit of the coast had been virtually saturated with holiday developments years before. Still, that was beside the point, and what Bill had actually done was get the land valued by two independent firms, and Randall had offered considerably more than the higher of the two figures so that Bill didn't see how he could do better by his client than accept.

'I shouldn't worry, Polly,' Thea said sympathetically. 'I'm sure nobody doubts Bill's integrity for a minute.'

'No, they couldn't very well, could they?' agreed Polly. 'But Bill's going through terrific guilts about disposing of the land and letting Randall make the whacking profit he'll get now that it is worth so much more because of planning permission. But I know that isn't what really interests you. No, what he's worried about now is that he didn't do the conveyance properly having done it at all. You see, it never occurred to him to wonder about that plot where the beach hut is. Randall has had it for as long as we've known the place, and the awful, awful thing is that it isn't specifically mentioned on the conveyance, so it really ought to belong to Miss Ferris still. Randall never had another conveyance of it, it appears. But you'll never guess what he's saying now.'

'What?'

'Well, he says that he has acquired a squatter's title, that means a title by adverse possession, and so it's his although he can't produce any title deeds.'

'What's so dreadful about that? Not that I really understand what you're talking about, I might add.' Polly got up and poured more apricot brandy for them both. They were sitting in her pastiche drawing-room: a comfortable mock-up of early Victorian elegance decorated with watercolours done by Bill's ancestors, floor-length cloths on small round tables and dried flowers galore. Fortunately it was relieved from being a tasteless joke by modern egg-shaped television set and some scattered plastic and wooden toys. The effect was charming and comfortable, and Thea glanced around appreciatively as she sipped the sticky liquid. She would have preferred whisky, but that was immured in the office end of the house with Bill, who was not exactly drinking his worries away but blunting them.

'No, it's all one of those ghastly bits of lawyers' muddle, things like Statutes of Limitation, and goodness knows how many conflicting cases trying to explain what they mean – just like everything else Bill talks about. Do you know, there just aren't any yes or no answers in the law. I've never heard Bill answer a legal question in less than three paragraphs and he always finished up saying "but the law is a little uncertain on that point" – it's fantastic. Of course, that's what makes us so comfortable!'

'I can see that there's profit in it. But surely someone

must know who the bit where the dig was belongs to? The local people or something? Because after all, I don't know whether you gathered, but the landowner stands to make literally thousands of pounds on that one find.'

'Not so much – you don't mean it? Oh golly, I must tell Bill that. He'll collapse.' Polly picked up the telephone receiver and pressed one of the row of little buttons on the base. 'We have to have this, with the office in the house,' she explained. 'Oh, darling. It's me. Look, come along to the drawing-room, and hear what I've just heard. Yes, it is important, and it's relevant too. Don't treat me like the little woman. And bring the whisky back with you.' She smiled at Thea as she put the receiver down and said, 'He does have this temptation to behave as though I were the pretty tatting nitwit this room deserves. I've been wondering whether to re-do it in a more emancipated style. Oh, here's Bill.' He came in carrying a silver tray, highly polished, on which were a silver-labelled decanter, some elaborately cut crystal tumblers and a nineteenth-century vintage soda siphon, such as an ancestor of his might have acquired by post from the Army and Navy stores when it started sending catalogues to outposts of civilisation. He didn't look like a lawyer, but like a jovial sailor worried by the wind, or a farmer by the state of the crops – a rubicund face and tweedy clothes and an obviously unaccustomed expression of anxiety.

'What is it, darling? I'm trying to go through the Pentowan estate again, and I really should get on with it. I've been wondering whether to get counsel's opinion, for my own peace of mind.'

'You mean pay for it yourself, not charge it to the client? You really must be worried. Well, you'd better hear what Thea said, then.' Thea apologetically told him about the probable market value of the crucifix, and he sank down on to the chaise longue.

'No, how awful,' he said. 'Polly, do you realise that I might have lost my client all that money? We'll have to fight it. It's professional negligence! My Lord,' he added, his accent in moments of stress, broadly Cornish, 'does Randall know that?'

'I don't know. Roger Thurstan might have told him,' Thea said. 'But I don't see how any of it can possibly be your fault. If Mr Cooper has really acquired a squatter's title, he must have been there long before you became the executor for old Miss Trevanion.'

'No, because the point is she was bats for the last years of her life and I managed her affairs. I should have done something about Randall. But he had that hut there before I took charge, when my father was still the senior partner, and I suppose I just assumed that he paid a peppercorn rent or something. I suppose it's possible that Miss Ferris knows the truth. But I never thought about it at all, which in the disgraceful part, because I often went there for fishing and picnics and things.'

'Yes,' Polly smiled secretly. 'And other things, I seem to remember. Darling, do stop scourging yourself and tell us sensibly. We're not lawyers, but it must be possible to explain it to somebody short of a Lord Justice and make it intelligible. Tell us what squatters' titles mean, and adverse possession and all that.' He took a cigar in shaking hands from a mahogany humidor, and lit it with a twisted paper spill from a jar on the mantelpiece, which he ignited from a log in the gleaming steel grate. Keeping up the archaic illusion must be pretty time consuming, Thea thought. Polly sat with her head bent over her embroidery as Bill went on,

'Well, it means that if you use someone else's land as though it were your own for long enough it becomes yours. You extinguish their ownership, in fact. And that's what Randall is claiming he's done.'

'You mean, I could just move in to Bunty's garden next door and grow potatoes and then it would become mine?'

'Not exactly, because she'd see you and protest about it. It has to be use which the owner doesn't complain about – he has to be ignorant, or at least acquiescent, which can't happen very often. And you have to be using it in such a way that the owner couldn't then do what he intended with it later. There was one case where a builder bought land and left it vacant for years till he could get started on it, and during those years a neighbour used it for her kids to ride their ponies on, or vegetable growing or something. Well, the judge said that the neighbour's claim to have acquired a squatter's title was impudent, and that her usage of the land was not inconsistent with the owner's enjoyment of the land for the purposes which he intended for it.'

'But after all, the Trevanions can't have intended to do anything with that bit of sand dune. It's just waste land, really. So how could Randall's hut be inconsistent with their intentions?' Polly asked.

'Well, just by being there and becoming a permanent building, I expect. And he did make that little picket fence – he was obviously using the land as his own. And the trouble is, that if the squatter ever admits to the owner that it really is the owner's land then he admits that he isn't busy acquiring a title to it – for instance, if he offers rent, or says that it's kind of the owner to let him use it. But in this case we just can't tell; after all, old Victoria's dead, and if Randall denies ever saying anything like that or getting her permission to use the land in the first place we can't prove that he's lying.'

'How many years do you have to use the land for?' Thea said.

'That's all governed by the Limitation Acts. There's normally a period of twelve years, and Randall has certainly been there longer than that. But it's all complicated again because of Miss Victoria's insanity. The limitation period is longer if the owner is insane at the time that the squatter dispossesses him; but I said that to Randall and he said that the old thing wasn't insane until much more recently. And that's another of my problems, because we never had her certified, there was no need as she was perfectly happy and looked after by those two old girls from the village. I mean, she wasn't really insane, she was just childish, and left everything to 'the grown-ups' to organise. But that wasn't any different from before, because she never did deal with her own business affairs, she always left everything to me, or to Father when he was alive.'

'And that's why you feel so responsible, I suppose,' Thea said sympathetically.

'Yes, yes. Because of course solicitors aren't supposed to be land agents really, it's not exactly my job to go plodding in person around my clients' estates even if I do manage their affairs. But you could say that I should have employed a qualified land agent. The Law Society might say so. And it's not as though I didn't know, anyway – I knew fine for years that Randall had his damned hut there. That's why I feel so guilty.'

'But, Bill,' Polly interrupted, 'it doesn't really make much difference whether Randall got that land by adverse possession as you call it, or whether he bought it when you sold to pay the death duties. The value of the ivory cross would be lost to the estate either way.'

Bill groaned. 'But suppose it wasn't,' he said. 'After all, we might have kept that patch out of the conveyance. And that's another worry. The planning permission. He must have known before he bought it that he'd get it, and if he applied before buying then he would have had to inform the owner. I'm absolutely terrified that I did get one of those forms ages ago, saying that he'd done so, and just forgot it. And if so then I sold it at a gross undervalue.'

'Oh, darling, nonsense. It's not the sort of thing you'd forget, I know you. No, probably if that is what happened, the form was sent to Miss Trevanion at Pentowan and thrown away unread. I'd have done that and I'm not even mental.'

'But if you could show that the old woman was insane more than twelve years ago anyway you'd be all right, wouldn't you?' said Thea. 'Have you sort of traced it back with her maids and the doctor and all the people in the village? It might be worth trying.'

'I don't know why you're so worried,' Polly said lightly. 'Just for Miss Rose Ferris? It doesn't seem worth while.'

'Oh, Polly, and you a lawyer's wife! She's my client, damn it. Wherever she is. That's another problem – what the hell has happened to her?'

'Still no sign of her?'

'No, and the police don't know whether to go on looking or not. Actually, I ought to go over there again. D'you want to come?'

'I can't, darling, it's Sigrid's evening at English lessons. Take Thea to keep you company. You'll go with him, won't you, Thea?' Thea agreed, and set off in Bill's solid car, which he would not drive off until he had inspected all the lights from the outside to make sure they were working, wiped the windows clear of any trace of condensation, and insisted on Thea strapping herself in. He was such a careful man that it was plain to see that any suggestion of professional slackness would be gall and wormwood to him. He drove with a firm and masterly hand, after all that; Thea had rather expected him to hug the crown of the road at twenty-five miles an hour. Hedges, houses and cows loomed as grey shapes in the gathering dusk, and low clouds scudded across the sky. The wind hit them fully as they drove over the spiny crest of the central moorland, and headed northwards towards Pentowan. Even Bill's heavy car felt less stable in the uneven gusts.

'I wonder whether I'll get used to the wind, living here,' Thea remarked. 'I don't think it's stopped for a minute since I came.'

'I don't notice it,' Bill replied. 'You might notice if there wasn't any. I always feel uneasy when I'm in London on fine days because it is so still.'

'I suppose it's bound always to blow by the sea. But I'll have to change my hairstyle – it's getting in my eyes,' Thea said, and tied a scarf over her head. Bill apologised, but his mind was elsewhere, and Thea gave up trying to divert him. Goodness knows, she had enough to think about herself.

X

Pentowan House was lit up, and there was a police car parked on the tarmac in front of it. Two policemen were in the drawing-room with two women. Bill greeted the sergeant by name, and introduced Thea. There was, it seemed, no sign of Miss Ferris anywhere.

'The thing is, sir, I don't quite know what I'm justified in doing,' the man said. 'We haven't any evidence that there is anything wrong here. This lady here, Miss Tyack from the village, says that there seems to be nothing out of place in the house – apart from what those two young people made free with. But it seems that nobody in the village went up to the house much since Miss Ferris moved in, no domestic help or anything like that. So it's perfectly likely that she has simply gone away for a few days.'

'But the stale food,' Thea said, 'and the way the house was open when I came here with Mrs Nankervis – surely she wouldn't have left it like that?'

'Well, miss, you'd be surprised what some people leave in their larders when they go away. We were called to break in to a house the other day because the neighbours couldn't stand the smell. The owners had gone off for ten days in Majorca and left the dog locked in the house with ten days' supply of meat. Chronic, that was. A heatwave too. And as for the open front door – Mr Nankervis here advised us of that. But Miss Tyack says that there are other ways into the house. Apparently there's a man called Phillips who lives near by who had regular access to it in the old days. He may even still have a key. So I've sent the constable out to look for him now.'

'It was a disgrace, that's what,' the woman called Miss Tyack burst out, to nods of agreement from the other woman; they looked like Tweedledum and Tweedledee, two round, dumpy bodies punctuating one another's thoughts, as though years of common employment, like marriage, had made them alike. 'They were always too good to that Batty Phillips up at the house here, letting him go rabbiting and come in and out and even paying him, not that he earned it. And there were my sister's boys out of work, couldn't find work down here then, something terrible the unemployment. And Miss Victoria wouldn't let Phillips go, not for anything. But we soon turned him out, once she started leaving things to us. Told him to keep his stupid face out of my kitchen, I did, and go back to his caravan. The smell of him; you wouldn't credit it. There were rats as big as cats around that caravan, and I'm telling no lie. Four of them there were, each as bad as the next, and Batty's the last one now. And the way they treated their old mum and dad. Laugh – I could have died when I saw how they'd fixed up their grave. Treated 'em like dirt when they was alive, they did, and then when they were dead, nothing too good for them. Granite gravestone, those green glass chips in it, oh lovely it is, and always putting flowers there on Sundays. Stolen, most likely, that's what I say. And we couldn't get rid of the man, could we, Emmy?'

'No, Maud, that we couldn't,' chorused the other woman.

'I've told him, and told him, I don't know how often I said to him, you keep out of here, Batty, I said. It's no use your coming looking for Miss Victoria now, there isn't going to be any more handouts from where those came from. You can write to the lawyer in Buriton, I said, that's you, sir, begging your pardon, and he'll tell you the same, so long as Miss Victoria's alive there's nothing more for you here. He'd come prowling around like some animal, looking in through the windows with his great china teeth bulging out of his mouth, fair gave us the creeps, didn't it, Maud, nasty unchristian, thieving creature that he is – I had to get my nephew to boot him off the premises once, I found him wandering around in the living-rooms, how he'd got in I do not know. And he's always bothering that gentleman that was let have a fishing shed, I do know. And those rabbits – I used to be as fond of a nice rabbit pie or pasty as the next person, but not since that nasty myxomatosis. I'd as soon eat a rat as a rabbit, and so I told him when he came along with the nasty creatures. Said they was a present for me, the cheeky fellow, for all he'd poached them off our land. Was lucky though, that was the only time I found him in the house, and that was when my nephew, the one who's a lecturer over to the college at Buriton, that was when he was here. Hurt his feelings to see his auntie in service, he said, such a kind, good boy he is. We're some proud of him, I can tell you, he'll be a professor soon, that's what he said the last time he come over, in the spring that was, he came with his baby and had a good tea with us. And he'll be on the wireless, and on the television too, once he starts getting on in the world.'

The police sergeant looked helplessly at the woman, and gestured Bill Nankervis over to the window with him. Thea followed, feeling that she had done her share by the verbal torrent, and stood beside her reflection in the dark glass. The wind was howling around the house now, it was like the sound effects in a radio play, and the sand was being blown noisily against the glass. There was a layer of it on the window sill already, although one could not see a gap for it to come through.

'I don't really know what to say, Sergeant Hocking,' Bill said. 'After all, you may well be right, and Miss Ferris has simply gone away for a few days. I don't think you can even charge those children with breaking and entering until we know whether she might really have given them permission to stay here, as they say. It's really impossible to tell, since there appears to be nobody who knows what clothes and suitcases there should be in the cupboards. When was she last seen, do you know?'

'Well, sir, it doesn't seem to be one of those gossipy villages, if you know what I mean. So many houses shut up all the winter, and different visitors every week throughout the summer.'

'Yes, I know what you mean. It's the county's tragedy. But someone must have seen her.'

'She went to the shop in the village a couple of times last week, but then one woman living alone, how often would you expect her in? And she might have gone shopping in one of the towns. It wouldn't really be surprising if nobody in Pentowan set eyes on her for months, that's just the trouble.'

'No, I realise that, the place is so terribly isolated. I was surprised that nobody from the excavations caught sight of her though. If she were here, you'd have thought she'd have come along to have a look at what was going on.'

'Well, sir, by all the signs she went away before it started. Isn't that what you told me?'

'It was the first full day when you came here with Polly, wasn't it, Thea? But people had been around quite a bit before then. Of course there's that great wall in the way, she wouldn't have had to notice anyone at all. I really don't know what to say.'

In the end Bill and the sergeant agreed that nothing much could be done. They could hardly put out missing person notices for a woman who might have simply gone away for a few days, even though Bill was eager to discuss the cross and its ownership with her. 'It's not as though I really had any position here now,' Bill said. 'I must remember that the owner isn't a crazy old woman whose affairs I see to. For all I know Miss Ferris has already employed somebody else as her solicitor. No, I don't see that I have authority to do anything.'

But Thea said to him, as they drove home again, 'It does make one uneasy, even though I can't put my finger on it. The place just doesn't feel quite right. I simply can't imagine the woman I saw on the train walking out of her house like that. She just wasn't that sort of person.'

'Oh, I didn't know you'd seen her. No, I agree, it does seem very peculiar, but I just don't see what we can do about it for the time being. She might come back any day from a holiday on the Costa Brava and be simply furious to discover that we've interfered at all. She probably wasn't used to housekeeping, and simply forgot that food you told me about. And as the police sergeant said, the doors could easily have been left open by Batty Phillips. I know him, he's as crazy as a coot.'

'It's a pity in a way that those two young people weren't there. I wouldn't put it past that girl to have ruined the site, you know. And if not that, at least they might have noticed something. What happened to them in fact?'

'Well, I turned them out. Though perhaps I was exceeding my authority, the girl did say that Miss Ferris wouldn't mind their being in the house. I suppose they went off to St Ives as they'd planned. It's always full of teenagers sleeping rough over there.' His voice held all the disapproval and scorn of the rate-paying citizen, but Thea had been through an anarchist phase when she was young and could remember the delight of being totally without possessions, responsibilities, inhibitions and duties. She could see the point of that kind of life style, which Bill Nankervis, in three-score years and ten, would never manage.

'Come in and see the photographs of the crucifix,' she invited, as he pulled up at the college lodge, but he refused curtly, and she regretted having reminded him of his own current cross; it was rubbing salt in the wound, she realised, even to have mentioned the Conservation Laboratories' photographs. None of those Bill had taken in the dusk at the excavation had come out, but she could not convince him that it was rather Roger's fault for making him try, than his own for having failed. In those conditions nobody could have taken a meaningful picture without special equipment.

She was relieved that he had not come in with her when she found Randall Cooper sitting on a window-sill in the passage outside her flat. He had come to see the photographs, and to hear what had been said at the laboratories, and she was obliged to invite him in, though it felt like disloyalty to poor tortured Bill. It was a surprise that the big, coarse-looking man seemed so moved by the intrinsic beauty of the object. He looked at the picture through a magnifying glass, exclaiming at the delicacy of the carving which portrayed faithfully the wool on the sheep's backs, and the decoration on the shepherd's crook.

'Seems a shame to have to sell it,' he said, putting the photograph down. 'Beautiful little thing. Imagine it just lying there waiting for us to find it all those centuries. Makes you think.'

'Yes, indeed,' she agreed. It was one of the clichés of

archaeological awareness, and she had grown out of that sort of emotion; quite good for one to be reminded of it, she thought, as she poured out whisky.

'What would you say it was worth?' he asked.

'It really isn't my province. You'd have to get it properly valued – or someone would have to, I mean. But there was something similar sold to the Victoria and Albert Museum in 1966, unprovenanced, but a bit more elaborate – a box, not a flat-backed cross – and I believe that fetched a good deal. I could get the V & A *Bulletin* from the university library and check.'

'Could you? I'd like that,' he said eagerly. 'Is it still open now?' She looked at his face and pinpointed in her mind what it looked: unsafe. If he could possibly have known that there would be money in it, she would not have hesitated to suspect him of arranging Rose Ferris's disappearance. Polly had warned her to protect her virtue from him, and he was not unattractive. Anyway, she could take care of herself, even with a man whose personality was like a battering ram. Feeling that she was playing with fire she admitted that the library was open till ten o'clock.

There were a few cars still parked outside the university library, but the place was eerily empty. A uniformed janitor sat at the turnstile, flanked by notices about closing time. Readers were warned in large capital letters that the library had a system of electric locks on all internal doors: they must, repeat must, leave the library within half an hour of the first bell and five minutes of the last, or be prepared to be incarcerated all night. The science fictional quality of this warning was reinforced by the extreme modernity of all the fittings: it was a brand-new building erected to combine maximum storage and working space with minimum cost of upkeep. There were various devices unfamiliar to

Thea, like conveyor belts for the books and stacks of movable shelves which slid on runners and pulleys.

Their shoes squeaked on the rubber floor as they walked past the shadowed stacks, and Thea found herself glancing nervously into each tabled recess as they passed, expecting goodness knows what to loom out of the darkness. Somehow Randall was not the right companion in a library, even one where you felt there might be something nasty around the next corner. He smelt too much of the world, there was nothing of a scholar's hesitancy and open-mindedness about him: even his huge square hands looked as though it was years since they had touched a hardbacked book.

The dead, conditioned, hot air muffled the scent of old books and printer's ink; but Randall gave out whiffs of sweat and tobacco. He was very large. When he put his arm around her shoulder it came down at an angle so that her ear rubbed against the hairy ginger tweed of his sleeve. Under the sleeve his arm was stonily hard, and his hand, on the thin material of Thea's dress, felt hot and dry.

She thought that it was odd that she did not in the least want to duck out from under his arm. Though she was wary of his intentions and motives, he was physically a comforting man to be embraced by. Thea was a small woman but none of the men she had known well had been very large. Sylvester himself, but for the originality of his expression, could have modelled as a Mr Average. It was nice to have this solid rock of a man at her side even in these unsuitable surroundings.

The Archaeology and Art History were together in a room at the far end of the fourth floor. Thea pressed the whole row of light switches and watched Randall's face as the sodium strips flickered into brilliance. His eyes were very blue, and he must have had red hair as a boy, though it was brownish grey now. He was looking around, self-confident and slightly amused. What did men like him think that universities were all about, anyway?

The *Bulletins* of the Victoria and Albert Museum were bound together in folders; she could feel his eyes watching her as she crouched down to the shelf where they were. He carried the pile she pulled out over to one of the tables, and she flicked through the indexes of the thick volumes. The one she wanted was published in 1966; it was almost illegible, because someone had spilled ink all over the cover and it had soaked through to the pages inside in a great blot. Thea noticed, as she peered at the obscured writing, that the last date stamp showed that this particular number had only been returned to the library at the beginning of this term, having been out for months. She pointed at the figure which had been paid for 'A rediscovered English reliquary cross', and felt pleased when she heard Randall draw his breath at the sight. It had fetched £40,000. She waited while he read the article with surprising attention, and then he stood upright and flicked the page a little scornfully.

'That's three times what I paid for all those acres at Pentowan,' he said. 'But then, what's money, after all? All comes out of our taxes.'

'You don't think it was money well spent?' she said.

'Special grants from the Treasury and all that? I suppose they'll be getting up appeals to find the lolly for our Cross too. Who am I to complain? It's better than some of the things the government waste it on, I guess.' Thea had always found it difficult to justify in argument the monetary value which was placed on pictures and *objets d'art*. Nor did she feel like indulging in the sort of discussion which was a commonplace of her tutorial classes. She closed the books, and left them on the table, and she and Randall began the long trek out of the library again. She wondered whether he would draw her into one of the shadowed recesses but he didn't; it must be a sign of either his maturity and self-confidence or of his lack of interest. Was he waiting to take her to bed? Or did he not want to?

Once at home, it proved to be the first; and a very good performer he was too, which was nice. She enjoyed herself as she might have done playing tennis, or indulging in any other pleasant physical pastime. It certainly meant no more to her than that; she felt neither affectionate, submissive not complaisant, whatever he may have hoped, but afterwards she lay beside him in her narrow bed feeling pleased and relaxed. He said in a faintly surprised voice, 'You're certainly liberated, aren't you, ducks?'

'What d'you mean? Am I too aggressive for you?'

'No no, lovely.' He massaged her skin with delicate movements of his huge hands. 'No, I mean, no tears, no saying what would your husband say, or my wife, or what must I think of you. You're almost like a man.'

She laughed. 'I suppose you mean that as a compliment. But I don't think I'm all that unusual for these days, am I? I just don't see my body as being all that important. What's the difference between your poking it for both our fun, and a doctor poking round in the same place and me hating it? I'm only involving my flesh. There are plenty of things I'd never say to you – that's what I regard as disloyalty, the mental intimacies.'

'So you aren't going to hate me or love me after this?'

'No more than before. We're strangers still, aren't we?'

'Well, let's stop being,' he said. 'There are lots of things we can do for each other.'

'Like this,' she said, showing him.

'Yes, and this; and this.' And a little later he said, 'You're a great girl, that you are.'

'And you're not all that small yourself.'

'You mean that I'm a big figure of a man. But I don't do too badly in other ways, as you'll discover if you stay down in Buriton. And money. Nobody would sneeze at a cut on that forty thou, would you think, old girl?'

'What I think is that you're counting your chickens.'

'Why, there's nothing wrong – oh, I know, you're thinking of poor old Bill Nankervis. Don't you worry about him. I'll establish my title to that plot of land all right.'

'Are you sure? Bill seemed to think there was plenty of doubt, I gathered.'

'Oh, he thinks he can show she was off her rocker before I started squatting there; he means well, of course. But not to worry about that, girlie, it's fixed. I've got all my witnesses sewn up, it's in the bag. Just in the bag.'

XI

Thea examined her face carefully in the glass the next morning. Such a pity that it wasn't true that sex made one's eyes sparkle and one's flesh clear. But she felt very well, and whistled as she dressed, only wincing a little because her breasts were sore where they had rubbed against the coarse curls of hair on Randall's chest. In the spirit of one accepting a dare, still wondering what he wanted of her, and how he expected to get it, she had agreed to go out to dinner with him that evening, and since he did not mention his wife, nor did she. One of her principles had always been never to become involved with the husband of one of her friends, and she expected Sylvester to observe the same rule in reverse. Not that she ever asked him. She assumed that he had the odd roll in the hay with the pretty girls he met at the television centre and elsewhere, but it was nicer not to know the details. As for her own indiscretions, which had in fact been few, she supposed that he was aware that they had happened from time to time. But she did not want him to be obliged either to make hideous scenes about them or to swallow all masculine pride by saying that he did not mind. In fact she always prided herself on the polite reticence which they had managed to maintain about unimportant physical details.

She laughed a little at the cerebral nature of her own responses. It was a source not only of pleasure but also of pride to her that she so much enjoyed herself in bed; it certainly wasn't a case of things of the mind being her substitute for a happy sex life, as other people were apt to assume. The all-round woman, she thought, zipping up her trousers, aren't I lucky. And yet at the back of her mind odd dissatisfactions were nagging. She tended to feel bilious and uneasy when she was not actually getting on with her own research and writing, and she had not done any of that for weeks. In fact she had taken great care to finish all half-done work and not to begin any new projects during the last few months, so that she would be able to start fresh at Buriton, but it made her almost more uneasy to have nothing that she should be writing than to have work that she should be doing now, and not to be hard at it. And there was the uncomfortable thought of her own department. She had such exalted intentions about it, and hoped to build up within three years one of the leading archaeological schools in the country. There again, her earlier optimism seemed quite misplaced. Every time she put her nose in to her office, she was faced with a full day's administrative work, chores which an office girl could do as well as she, but which consumed all the time and energy she had. Things might become easier once the term was under way. But then there was the problem of Roger. What sort of academic improvement could she initiate with him as her senior lecturer? His incompetence and hostility would sabotage any plans. And how far would the university support her in her sweeping reforms? There had been no suggestion since her arrival that money would be forthcoming even for an adequate library, let alone the other expensive projects and equipment she had planned for. Perhaps one was better as a junior in someone else's department, she thought sadly, her mood having swung in two minutes from elation to gloom; she was not sure that she could cope with all this at all. She watched herself cynically in that remaining part of her mind which was always coldly aware of her own absurdity: her *doppelgänger*, her saving grace, the seventh section of the soul which never slept or merged.

Good hard work is what you need, my girl, she prescribed. And after breakfast, she went along to Helen Eliot's rooms, to make a start on her papers as the Principal had asked.

It had all been tidied and cleaned, and only the brightness of one of the corners of the brass fender reminded one that against it Miss Eliot's temple had been crushed. The room seemed cold and unloved, only two days after Helen Eliot had filled it with her own vitality, although all the same things were displayed and the only tangible difference was that the grate held a fan of white paper instead of the scented logs. Thea shivered, though the radiator was full on, and felt like a burglar as she crossed to the writing desk. There was a half-completed foolscap page of handwriting, a list being transcribed of vestments from a sixteenth-century book on domestic economy. Thea looked at the filing cabinet which stood beside the mahogany bureau. Its drawers were labelled in the same elegant script, and everything was orderly within. Thea leafed at random through one of the files; at the beginning was a note which read:

'To my executor: this file is material for my book on the medieval housewife, published 1966: bonfire material now.' In fact all the files which she opened had similar directions, and most of them seemed to be relics of old and completed work. Some gave addresses of other workers in the same field to whom they should be passed and some were to be deposited in the college library. It was a display of consideration and efficiency which moved Thea almost to tears: how typical of the old girl, and how unusual. There certainly would not be much for Thea to do here, which was as well since she had dreaded the chore. It was turning out instead to be a labour of love.

There was one file which Thea looked round for with a personal interest; she wanted to read again the description that Helen Eliot had shown her of the ivory crucifix which sounded so like the one from Pentowan. All the more since hearing Helmuth Muller's doubts she was forced to wonder whether somehow the two objects were in fact one. It should not be difficult to find, though Thea could not see it in the cabinet. Probably it was still lying around somewhere. It must have been taken out on the Monday to show Roger Thurstan. The old lady had said she would ring him, and he had mentioned having seen her that day. It had been in a blue folder, Thea remembered, but she could not see it lying anywhere in the piles of books and papers on all the flat surfaces. She peered a little reluctantly into the bedroom. This looked far more old-personish than the sitting-room. Here the bed was high, the carpet thin, the wardrobe imitation Chinese lacquer, and there was the indefinable smell of the clean old. A basin and ewer stood on a marble wash-stand and there were thick lace curtains matching the bedspread; a white shawl hung over the end of the bed and a pair of sheepskin slippers waited on the small woolly mat beside the bed, a homemade one with flower patterns, in bright colours. Made by one of the twenty-three godchildren, perhaps? The room was adequately comfortable but it made Thea feel, without knowing why, her first and only twinge of pity for Helen Eliot.

Anyway, the blue folder was not in here either, in fact there were no books or papers in the room. Where could it be? Oh well, one could ask Roger later on, he might even have taken it away with him. The matter was not important.

She went into the department after lunch. The dull

letters requiring answers and forms to fill in had piled inexorably up. It was like the labour of Sisyphus: she would never be able to clear the in-basket, and say that the job was finished. Thank goodness for the new secretary, who was helpful and efficient, and even understood the complexities of arranging timetables. There was, as usual, no sign of Roger Thurstan.

Thea dressed with particular care that evening. Although she was happy to leave Randall's wife unmentioned, and felt few qualms about her, since if it was not one woman with a man like that it would be another, and Thea at least would never prod him towards divorce, still she wanted to show herself in a favourable light if he thought of comparing them. Without having met Mrs. Cooper it was hard to know how best to show up the difference, but her King's Road latest seemed sure not to have reached Buriton yet. Randall had such an impassive face that it was impossible to tell whether he approved of it, but he handed her tenderly into the passenger seat of his large car; and she hoped that a veneer of social assurance concealed the rather stimulating mixture of curiosity and uneasiness she felt.

They were going to eat in St Ives and Thea enjoyed the drive across the peninsula. When she first saw it, and since coming down here to live, she had felt faintly uneasy in this unfamiliar landscape of rocks and scrub, with tiny fields bounded by huge-bouldered dry-stone walls. Not that she was the sort of person to start thinking about pixies, ghoulies and ghosties, or any of the imaginative bogies which more sensitive characters might shrink from. Her reaction was the far more matter-of-fact one of a person who knew something about land economy; it was hard to see how any farming in these conditions could be at more than subsistence level, even when eked out by the profitable annual crop of tents and caravans; it felt like seeing a display of the life styles of the peasants whose material remains she had spent years studying. But increased familiarity made her realise how wrong her first reactions had been. The farm houses might seem small but most were meticulously kept up, with brightly painted woodwork and huge television aerials. The animals in the fields were glossy and plump, and it became clear that the size of the fields had been dictated not by poverty but by the distance to which one could roll the boulders when clearing the ground in the first place. Even the tents acquired a certain charm when one looked at them without prejudice: a brightly coloured decoration on the various shades of green, like a Grandma Moses painting. And the sea, visible or audible from many places, and something of which one was always aware, completed the picture like a well-chosen frame.

She gazed about her filled with pleasure and benevolence, unembarrassed by silence; and the view of St Ives was delightful. In the lucid glow of the fine evening the little town might have been a Mediterranean fishing port, with rows of ships anchored in the enclosed harbour, brightly painted houses and a few fishing smacks sailing off towards the sunset. It was a charming sight, and she said so.

'I thought you'd like it,' Randall agreed. But her liking diminished when she inspected the place more closely. It would be lovely, one could see that, if it were not so crowded, so exploited, so apparently given over to its own financial exploitation. They seemed to be driving down the hill into a miasma of fish and chips, rock and candy floss; and not a house to be seen which did not welcome bed-and-breakfasters, not a shop without its rack of Midland-made souvenirs.

However, the dinner was good; and the evening view

across the bay, as they stood looking down upon the harbour afterwards, was unspoilable. There were fewer people around now, though even in the chilly dusk some boys and girls were in the sea. Randall tucked Thea's hand in his arm, and they strolled down towards the waterfront. The paddlers were coming off the beach now, towards their trousers which were draped on the railings above the beach. Thea sniffed cautiously, and Randall laughed.

'Don't kid yourself that's ozone,' he said. 'Something not nearly so nice,' and Thea looked with less favour on the seagulls which swooped and whirled around the shallow water. 'Nothing those birds like better than a nice bit of muck,' he said. 'Pity they don't go for the human scum too.'

'What do you mean?'

'All those kids down there – those layabouts. Just look at them, lazy-good-for-nothing bums. Don't know why they don't chase them out of town with police dogs.' She glanced up to see whether he was joking, but there was no smile on his jutting face, and she was automatically shocked. 'Oh, I know you,' he said indulgently. 'A pinko-grey lib-lab, that's you. I've seen that husband of yours spouting often enough to know that. But you don't meet ordinary people's problems in your safe telly world, or in your learned ivory towers. It's easy enough to talk about tolerance when you don't have anything to put up with yourself.'

'You do surprise me,' she said truthfully.

'I dare say I do. It'll be a long time since you met an ordinary businessman like me, I'll be bound. But I know more about what life's about than you do, girlie, I'll tell you that. And young louts like those ruin the town's trade, and without trade where would the nation be?' He looked with loathing and she with interest at the group of boys and girls who were chattering and shrieking at one another as they pushed their wet limbs into jeans. They had a few motor-bikes leaning up against the railings and wore their generation's uniform hairstyles and clothes – red rags to bull-like men like Randall.

'They've had to pull down the bus shelters, to stop the kids sleeping in them,' he said angrily. 'And they steal anything they can lay their hands on. And take drugs. Scum of the earth, they are, and they think they own it.' The young people ignored anyone who was not part of their gang, and Thea noticed that solid citizens who walked by gave them a wide berth: as though, she thought, they were people to fear.

'They don't look all that different from some of my students,' she said.

'No need to tell me that. I've seen that collection we keep in luxury for three years. Bring back national service, I say.'

'And hanging, and the cat-o'-nine-tails?'

'Yes, why not? We're too soft nowadays.' She withdrew her hand from his arm, suddenly finding it not funny but disgusting.

The gang had been standing in a noisy crowd, flaunting their indifference to the passers-by. Now they seemed to have agreed on something to do, and they wheeled around and moved off, like a flock of starlings in their marshalled action. And yet it was to escape discipline that they were here. But group identity was not oppressive when one had chosen it; and Thea looked to see whether it was apparent which of the identical-looking creatures was the leader of them – though it was hard enough to tell which was male and which female, at the moment.

But suddenly Thea saw a face which she did know: it was the girl who had been at Pentowan, loping along hand in hand with a long thin youth, their heads down and hair trailing. She called, 'Julie! Julie Robertson!' and the girl looked round briefly. Then she yelled something, laughing, and the whole group took to their heels, and raced whooping into a narrow alley.

'Who was that?' Randall asked.

'It's the girl who was at Rose Ferris's house. I don't expect you know about her. But I'd like to have a word or two with her. Where do you suppose they've gone?'

'Lord knows. Not far enough, to my way of thinking. Come on, we're not going to chase after them now. Let's not spoil our evening.' He hugged her shoulder in what was becoming a habitual gesture, but now for a new reason it made her feel uneasy and almost guilty. How amusing, she thought, that she should be quite unaffected by standard womanly emotions, as Randall himself had commented, but that discovering the alien quality of his mind should have made her feel that they had no right to mix their bodies. She did not suppose that Mrs Cooper would understand or believe in her scruples. But she drew away from Randall, as though he had taken a liberty to which he had no right.

There was a police patrol car parked half-way up the hill, and she stopped to speak to the driver, a fat man who could hardly be older than the girl she was looking for. He did not know where the crowd of youngsters had gone, but he said they sometimes slept on the beach, sometimes they went out to the moors and took shelter among the outcrops of granite. 'They aren't made welcome here,' he said smugly.

'I can see that,' Thea replied in a dry voice. They were standing beside a public bar, and pasted on its door was a notice reading 'No beatniks or undesirables allowed in'. 'How do they tell who's undesirable?' she asked.

'Oh, it's the clothes, and the beards, madam. You can see

at a glance.'

'Any indication of not conforming, in fact,' she said to Randall.

'That's it. Quite right too – shows an undisciplined mind otherwise.'

'Oh look – there they are.' The gang was coming down the narrow street towards them now, in three arm-linked chains across the street, singing. There was a queue of cars behind them, but they did not move aside. Thea looked round to see that the young policeman had discreetly driven off in time to pretend he had not seen them. Thea stood back in a doorway: she did not want Julie Robertson to run away at the sight of her again. 'Come along, Thea,' Randall urged.

'No – I want to wait for that girl.'

'Well, I'm damned if I'll hang around waiting for a crowd of layabouts. I'll meet you in the car when you've had your say.' He swung off into a side street, and Thea suddenly realised that both he and the policeman had actually been afraid to confront the group. She searched her conscience to see whether she were afraid herself: it would, she felt, be a shameful emotion. But in fact she was not afraid. What could they do but laugh at her? But then, it was probably ridicule that men like Randall most feared.

As a matter of fact, some of them had rather attractive faces. They were all bonily thin, and smelt pretty revolting, but they did not have the weaselly pale faces which their London counterparts always displayed. There was something to be said for sleeping on beaches and moors after all, and living on milk even if it was stolen. Their eyes were bright, and they seemed rosy and vigorous.

Here was the girl. Thea jumped out of her doorway and grabbed her by the arm. 'Just ten minutes, Julie,' she said.

'Honestly, I only want to ask you some harmless questions.' The whole group turned and stopped. She smiled round at them. 'I'm not the enemy,' she said. They stared at her beadily, giggling a little. It was like being surrounded by large dogs, there would be no trouble so long as they did not sense fear or uncertainty. The tallest boy, who was draped with a blanket and three musical instruments, said,

'OK, Jule, see you at the usual.' And they all marched off again, leaving the girl standing warily beside Thea, her eyes fixed on the ground. Her boy-friend had waited too, and Thea said, 'You must be Sid. Can I give you a drink or some coffee or something? Where could we go, just for a little while?'

'They don't let us in, the places here,' the boy muttered.

'Nonsense. They've no right to refuse. Come along.' She pointed to a Wimpy Bar across the road.

'They say we keep the other customers away,' Julie said.

'Well, maybe you do, if the whole lot of you go in at once. But you'll be all right with me, and I expect you're hungry.' The Wimpy Bar also had a notice about undesirables pasted to its door, but Thea fixed the waitress with a quelling glance, and led the way to a table.

Hamburgers and coffee were treated like manna, and for a few minutes the two young people gobbled as though the meal were their first and last. They refused cigarettes a little scornfully.

'I'm not trying to get at you, honestly,' Thea began. 'I've no official status, I'm just nosy. So you won't get into trouble for anything you say to me. But I do want to know about that time you were at Miss Ferris's house. Did you see any signs of her, in fact? The thing is that she seems completely to have disappeared. Which was the first night you were there? Was it Saturday? That was the day that we met you there.'

The girl looked at her boy-friend blank-faced, and then she giggled. 'Oh, we took you in,' she said. 'I only rang the bell in case she'd come back. We'd been there the night before too.'

'You mean there was no sign of her on the Friday either? Which day was it you first turned up at Pentowan, then?'

'It was on Thursday evening. But we didn't break in, honest. The door was open the way it was when you went there. But there wasn't any sign of old Rosie. We hung around for a bit and then we went for a swim and then we thought we might as well wait in the house for her. I told you she'd have been pleased to see me. And then we just stayed.'

'Where?'

'Well, we sort of camped in one of those rooms downstairs that first night. In case she came back late you know. But there wasn't any sign of her so after that we thought we'd be safe in one of the bedrooms,' she said, giggling again, but staring blatantly and defiantly at Thea.

'What did you think had happened to her?'

'Oh, gone for a swim and drowned or something. We didn't much care.'

'There were footprints in the sand dunes, though,' Sid said.

'Oh, fancy yourself as a detective, don't you,' Julie jeered. 'Footsteps indeed – course there were. There was that man poking around in his potty dig, wasn't there – he didn't fly to it, you know.'

'Well, I only thought I'd mention it, that's all,' Sid said.

'What do you mean?' Thea asked. 'Nobody was digging on the Thursday. Is that the day you're talking about?'

'Yeah. Took us two days to get down from the smoke. So

it must have been the Thursday. Been raining all day, we was soaked. So we went in the sea for a bit to finish off the job but it was too cold for Jule here. And then I raced her back through the sand dunes to the old bag's place.'

'And you saw someone at the dig? Wasn't it just the owner of the beach hut going fishing?'

'Fishing with a spade? What d'you think? An' it weren't that old man, anyway. Much more switched on. Jeans, you know, and a boutique shirt.'

'It must have been Mr Thurstan getting things ready.'

'Could be,' the boy answered, bored. 'Anyroad, we stayed in the house that night. The water was hot then too. Jule even washed her hair. As though the rain hadn't been doing it all day.'

'It was all sweaty from the skid-lid,' she said defensively.

'All right, I don't care, all the same to me. Only I was afraid the old bag might come in in the middle of it.'

'She wouldn't have minded, I'm sure she wouldn't. She was fond of me,' the girl repeated.

'I'll bet.' He laughed derisively and looked sideways at Thea. We're both thinking the same thing, she thought; poor Rose Ferris.

'Have you no idea where she is now, then?'

'Ain't there any sign of her at all, then?' Julie asked. She used slang conscientiously, but it obviously did not come naturally, and Thea remembered having been told that Rose Ferris had taught at quite a smart school. What were this girl's parents about, for heaven's sake?

'No, she hasn't been back. You left on the Monday, did you?'

'Yeah, day before yesterday it was. But we thought she'd just gone away. People do. We did ourselves, in London.

Nothing to get all up tight about. She a friend of yours, or what?'

'No, I told you,' Thea said. 'It's nothing to do with me. I'm just interested. I'll tell you something else I wondered about. Remember, I really mean it about just wondering. You were there on the Saturday night, weren't you – I suppose you didn't go over to the dig, did you?'

'No. Why should we? Anyway, we went out Saturday night, took in a movie and some fish and chips. Didn't get back till late.'

'So you wouldn't have seen anyone at the dig site?'

'Wouldn't have been interested,' Sid said. Julie added,

'There was someone there though. There was a car parked by the end of the lane.'

'What sort of car?' Thea said.

'How should I know? We aren't interested in cars, are we, Sid? Anyway, we didn't go on the beach just to look at old cars.'

'Did you notice, Sid?'

'No, like Jule says, we aren't interested in bourgeois pollution. Oh well, it was some sort of old estate car, I think. 'Cause I did look to see if there was anyone in it with the back seat flat. But there wasn't, just a lot of old muck. Kids' jerries and that.'

'Someone went and ruined the excavation site that night,' Thea told them, but they were not interested. It really did not seem likely that they had done it themselves.

They were sitting on the edge of the bench waiting to be allowed to go. Then Sid realised he needed no permission, and he pulled Julie to her feet.

'We'll be off, then, if that's all,' and without thanking Thea for the food they ran from the café, and down the hill to find their friends.

The girl at the cash desk looked curiously at Thea. 'You a reporter or something? Getting local colour?'

'Is that what it looks like?'

'Can't think why else you'd be talking to the likes of them. Or are you their mum?'

Thea stumped furiously up the hill. Next thing, she'd be addressed as Gran by bus conductors. Her reflection looked unchanged to her in the shop windows, but always before friends had expressed surprise that even Clovis could be her son. Bloody little town, bloody intolerant provincials in it. She wished she could grow a beard herself just to show them all: why, half her friends in London would be refused admission to the local pubs and cafés if they were judged by their clothes and hairstyles, including Sylvester's editor who looked like an anaemic golliwog, and her own former boss, who had worn a straggling beard and had not owned a tie for years except one on which a naked lady displayed her private parts in silk appliqué.

Randall was waiting in the car, patient and unreproachful. He was half-way through a cigar, and told her that he was never bored; always had something to think about. But Thea was too cross to make the right responses and did not encourage him to tell her about his thoughts. If they were what she supposed, she did not allow him to put them into action either, but thanked him for her meal without inviting him in, and perhaps the worst thing to do to someone who had expected to make love to her, held out her hand for him to shake on the doorstep of the Barbican College porter's lodge. To his credit, he did so in such a way that the watching night porter could think none the worse of either of them, and Thea felt positively ashamed as she went alone to her flat.

XII

Lonely in bed. Matrimony no training for this life. Buy a plastic man? Joke – how to explain to Clovis if he found it? Need a warm back to hold, a warm arm to be caressed by. Pad sides with pillows and hot-water bottles. No substitute. Any body better than none. Should have brought Randall Cooper in. But one's pride ... couldn't let someone who said that sort of thing ... cutting off nose to spite face because he never realised that she minded so much. Probably thought she'd had a headache. Or the curse. Can't lie here thinking that any man would do. Theodora, stop it. Giving substance to hostile suspicions. Be Roger Thurstan next at this rate. Handsome. But probably no good in bed. His wife wouldn't be quite so discontented otherwise. Or would she? What did they want out of life, anyway? To be rich and famous and successful. Worldly ambition. Silly. All very well for me to talk. Probably want it myself if I hadn't got it. Go to any lengths, I dare say. But Sylvester wouldn't be the same person if he wasn't successful. I'd be living with someone else. Would I leave him? Might do. Can't tell what I'm capable of. What would the Thurstans do? Lady Macbeth type, Celia Thurstan? Would she egg him on? Probably not to do things specifically, just by complaining. Ghastly woman. Wonder what she's thinking about me? Wax images and pins. But I feel all right. Expect she just eggs him on by displaying her discontent. He's too wet to do anything about it. No fear of knives in my back. Anyway he must know it wouldn't help. Nobody'd ever make him a professor. Unless he makes his name now with the crucifix find. Probably looks marvellous on the box. Should have watched.

Oh God, that was two a.m. striking. If Clovis was here he could come in to warm me up. Not so cold though. Just lonely. I can hear the sea. High tide. What was Roger doing digging at Pentowan on Thursday? Quite late it must have been. Didn't stop raining till the evening. Nice smell, the rain down here. Good for one's complexion. Look at Polly Nankervis's, so smooth and English rose-ish. Couldn't say the same for Celia Thurstan. Probably leaves poor Roger to wheel the babe in the rain. What was he doing that evening? The boy did say he was actually digging with a spade. Not just laying out or measuring. That pit perhaps, the one they called James's pit? But why, for goodness' sake? Not much method in his madness...

Wind getting up outside again. Gets caught in the corner of the building and howls like dervishes. Wonder if it's windy in the Far East where Sylvester is. Don't expect he's alone in bed. Is it night time there? Some pretty dusky maiden...

Feels funny without Clovis. He seems to love it with all those other boys. Pity we never had any more. He's so sweet ... enthusiastic. Loved it digging the other day. Terribly excited about that crucifix. Perhaps they'll call it the Clovis cross. Funny how he found it, never anything like that on my digs. Lucky Roger. Make his name with four inches of walrus tusk. Wonder whose it was. Some big-wig of the Dark Ages, buried with his trappings. Dust to dust ... must have fallen down through the rib cage on to the vertebrae ... did they know that would happen when they buried him in full regalia? Rather a waste ... nice for the archaeologists though ... Miss Eliot and the nitrogen cycle.

Rather be burned and scattered myself.

Helmuth Muller, so affectionate. Wonder whether he'd be nice to have in here now? All on the surface. Probably a cold fish really, just oils the wheels of social intercourse. Be outraged if I invited him into my bed ... more interested in the incense in the cracks of the cross than in what I smell of ... funny that there was incense resin there ... funny that description Helen Eliot showed me ... must ask Roger Thurstan about it. Not my worry really but I am worried. And about Rose Ferris. What on earth has happened to her? Oh, to sleep. Sleep and his brother death. Too much death round here. To sleep, perchance to dream ... wish I could. Dream of some nice man. Once had an orgasm from a dream ... woke Sylvester up to tell him. Macbeth hath murdered sleep. That would be Roger Thurstan, if Celia's Lady Macbeth. Roger Thurstan hath murdered sleep ... Oh God!

Thea switched her light on, and went to make herself a cup of tea. She sat and read *Sense and Sensibility* until four o'clock and then dozed uneasily until dawn. A bad night.

And she was greeted by a bad day too: no letter from Sylvester but a list of confessions from the tenants of the house in Canonbury of what they had already broken. A cheque was enclosed, but it seemed no satisfactory substitute. The wind she had heard rising in the night was blowing hard now, stripping the leaves prematurely off the trees and flattening the last flowers of the summer. There were a few large ships sheltering in the bay, but the wind was from the north-west, and the porter said knowledgeably that most would have run in to St Ives Bay for safety.

After such a bad night Thea felt nervous and ill-at-ease. She was unreasonably anxious about Clovis: would they make sure he was all right at school, keep him from the edge of cliffs and from standing under rotten elm trees? She could not bear the thought of going to her room in the university. The wind would be making banshee noises in the architect's artistic crevices, and even on the first floor she would feel the whole tower shaking. It was all very well to be assured that high buildings were safer if they were made to sway with the wind, but it was a hateful sensation from the inside. She stayed in her own flat and spent an unsatisfactory morning writing overdue personal letters, and at lunch time decided to try the university Staff Club for the first time.

Among the multitudes of brochures she had received when first in Buriton had been a glossy puff for this handsome new addition to the university. It had been provided by a millionaire from Arizona whose grandfather had left Buriton to make his fortune but insisted that his family remain loyally Cornish. The aim was that there should be a neutral meeting ground for members of staff in all the disciplines and of both sexes. He had said that he wanted the dons to get a feeling of 'togetherness' but it had been more pompously rephrased in the university's literature. It was an unusual asset for a university which was based on the collegiate system, but should have been a good idea. Unfortunately, Thea had already been told, it did not work. The place was packed out at lunch-time with non-teaching members of staff, from librarians to junior typists, and student protests two years before had forced the senate to allow student membership also, as it was regarded by activists as discriminatory.

Then last year there had been another protest, this time less active but equally effective, by the wives of members of staff of all grades, who demanded the right to use the building as their husbands did, and the place, according to one scornful Barbican College don, was nothing more these days than a social club for the idle citizens of Buriton, much used by them during the summer because the other facilities of the town were packed out with tourists, and because membership of the Staff Club allowed access to the university's tennis courts and playing fields.

The place had been decorated in elegant colours and materials, which eighteen months of over-use had already rendered shabby. But there were some interesting pictures on the walls acquired as an enlightened investment, and Thea was favourably impressed by the atmosphere. She certainly did not feel shy or out of it, although there were, at first sight, no faces she knew. It all seemed rather lively and entertaining, and she sat down with gin and the *Illustrated London News*, feeling more cheerful than for many hours. She did not read the magazine, but looked over it at everybody else. It was impossible to tell from the way they looked whether people were teaching members of staff or extras. Would the rule that the shabbier the cleverer hold good here?

There was the professor of geography. She had met him when she was interviewed for her own chair. He came over and sat down at the same low table.

'Hullo, remember me? I'm Alfred O'Connor. Nice to see you here – you don't mind if I join you? I've a friend with me too.'

'Not at all, delighted. I was just feeling out of it – not a single other face I know. Oh yes, there's one: do you know Randall Cooper, standing over there?'

'Not a member of the university, is he?' Professor O'Connor said with disfavour, watching as Randall waved at Thea. He was standing with a jabbering and heavy drinking crowd, all of whom were on loudly familiar terms with the barman. 'Well, and how are you settling down, Professor Crawford?'

'Quite well, thank you. I haven't completely found my way about yet, of course. But life seems to be full of incident.'

'Oh, so I've been hearing. Quite a boost for that young man. But I hear there are complications – you'll have noticed how people talk here!'

'Oh yes. Inevitable in any small community, isn't it? But I don't know what's happening about my colleague's discovery. I'm finding it all a little worrying, to tell you the truth, though it's not really my pigeon.' Thea started violently and spilled some of her drink as a kiss landed on the top of her head. She turned round to see an old London friend, and jumped up to kiss him warmly back, feeling a little as one Eskimo might when meeting another in a tropical jungle. 'Esmond – what on earth? How lovely to see you – but how come?' Esmond Smith sat down between Thea and Alfred O'Connor, after carefully wiping up the spilt gin with his handkerchief.

'I've come down to do a feature,' he said. 'Guess what about?'

'I can't think,' Thea said. 'But how extraordinary, and why didn't you tell me? And where's Diana?'

'Baby-bound. The second one is due in a month, didn't you know? And I was going to come and see you naturally, not to mention that I need to for my feature. I've heard from Sylvester too.' Thea turned politely to Alfred O'Connor, to explain.

'Esmond and my husband are in the same line,' she said. 'And now they work for the same paper. My husband used to be in television.'

'So Mr Smith told me,' the geographer replied. 'He's

been picking my brains all the morning about conditions in the sand dunes here, not that I'm much of a soil scientist, as I told him.'

'Sand dunes? Oh, Esmond, you haven't come down because of the ivory crucifix, have you?'

'Indeed I have. Make a lovely feature for this weekend. You'll have to let me have a photograph of Clovis with a trowel to put in with it.'

'I'll do no such thing. And surely an article would be a bit premature? You must have heard about the dissensions?'

'Treasures always bring quarrels in their train,' Esmond replied sententiously. 'Of course I've heard about it. I talked to Sylvester on the telephone the day before yesterday and he said that from your letters it was clear that you were living in the middle of a detective novel, thrills daily.'

'Am I? I've never read one so I wouldn't know,' Thea said.

'Never read one? What never?'

'No, I don't really read novels much. Except Jane Austen in trains. And some of the early Victorian ones like Susan Ferrier. But it's rather a waste of time, I'd have thought.'

Esmond seemed to have been completely sidetracked from his original questions. He asked,

'Do you honestly mean that you've never read a modern novel in your life? I can't think how you manage it.'

'Well, they just don't interest me. I have a very concrete mind, you know.'

'Fascinating,' Esmond murmured. 'Don't be hurt if I say so, but it must make your knowledge of life so very limited. You must be unaware of anything which is outside your own experience. Not that I'm saying your own experience of life is narrow, I'm sure you make the most of your opportunities, but think what you don't know about.'

'Do you mean you read light fiction for its documentary qualities? That's a new idea to me,' Professor O'Connor said.

'No, not entirely of course, but you pick up something you didn't know about other people's way of life from every word. Even if it's only about the author's way of life. But that explains why Sylvester was worried about you, Thea my dear.'

'Is he? I didn't know.'

'He thinks you're getting mixed up in things that you just aren't aware of. Because your own experience is of people being rational and virtuous. Of course you could just say that all journalists are policemen at heart.'

'I don't read light novels either,' said Alfred O'Connor. 'Never have the time. When one is doing important work – what one might call enlarging the frontiers of knowledge, writing papers with objective importance and validity – well, one loses the taste for trivia. I'm glad to hear you feel the same, Professor Crawford.'

'All right,' Esmond said laughing. 'I grant you that on the day of judgement one scholar will be weighed against at least three journalists like me. You can rest secure in the conviction that your work is of superior importance to mine. But you do the work in an imperfect world, I'm afraid. Not all your colleagues are selfless goodies untormented by worldly desires. Which is why I'm here.'

'Oh dear,' Thea sighed. 'It's the money, I know. Nobody would look twice at the crucifix if it wasn't for its saleroom value – except for unworldly academics like me, Esmond. You'll never get anyone to believe that archaeologists really are more interested in its implications.'

'Some,' said Esmond. 'But the thing's only been above

ground for less than a week and I've already heard from Sylvester about discoveries, dissensions and death. Your letters to him seem to be full of drama.'

'I'm vexed that he's had this rush of protection to the head,' Thea answered. 'Quite uncalled for. Just because I tell him about the interesting things and not the dull intervals there's no need to assume that they are all connected. I shall have to turn my letters into something more like Pepys' diaries and tell him about my beds and breakfasts.'

'No, I think it's another way of showing that the onlooker sees most of the game,' Esmond said. 'That's why I enjoy my job so much. Look, there are some of the protagonists on their way over here now, I believe. Isn't that the man you pointed out to me earlier, Alfred?' A group of men was edging through the crowd. There was Randall, massive in ginger tweed, smiling and nodding in all directions like a film star. Bill Nankervis followed him, but though he too must have known most of the people in the room he looked anxious and preoccupied; and walking beside him was Roger Thurstan. Roger broke straight in to speech, without waiting for introductions or greetings.

'We wanted to see you, Alfred. I want you to bear out what I've been saying to Randall Cooper here. Not that he denies it, but just to make sure, you know. Do you remember at the pre-sessional party at the Vice-Chancellor's, about a fortnight ago, just before I started digging at Pentowan, Randall agreed that if I found anything valuable on his land he'd go halves with me?'

'I do remember your saying something about it, yes. Though I didn't take it seriously.'

'Wouldn't stand up in a law court,' Bill said gloomily. 'No intention to create legal relations, I shouldn't think.'

'Well, it doesn't really matter.' Randall sat down beside

Thea and beckoned a waiter. 'You don't mind if we join you? Same again all round, please, Howard.' Thea thought, he's the sort of man who always knows the waiters by their first names. Randall gave her a brief glance which was so extraordinarily intimate that she blushed, and glanced at Esmond to make sure he had not noticed. Then Randall went on, 'I'm not arguing. Looks as though the thing's worth enough for both Roger and me to get a nice windfall.'

'You'll have to show it's yours first,' Thea said, since it was evident that Bill was too acutely embarrassed by the unconventional surroundings to contribute his legal mite. He was twisting his glass round and round in his fingers and staring at his feet: there should have been a balloon labelled 'without prejudice' floating above his head, she thought.

'Oh; little doubt about that, I'm glad to say,' Randall said. 'No skin off old Bill's nose either for all he looks so sad about it. After all, his client's not around and he never met her in the first place. No, my need is greater than hers, ha ha.' He turned to Alfred O'Connor and Esmond Smith with expansive friendliness. 'It's a nice little plot we're talking about, where the treasure came from. And I'm lucky enough to have acquired a title to it by adverse possession – what you call a squatter's title. Praise be for the English legal system, what?' He was not apparently drunk, but only the shrewdness in his eyes showed that: it was a convincing performance otherwise of the man who says more than he should because he has had a glass more than is good for him.

'I thought there was some question of Miss Victoria Trevanion's sanity at the time,' Thea asked and added, 'I gathered that the period of twelve years squatting only applies if the original owner was sane at the beginning of them?'

'She was sane enough then,' Randall said. 'Fortunately I can prove that. Can't I, Roger old boy?' Roger Thurstan shook his hair violently from his eyes. He said,

'Oh yes, I'd say so. One of my old aunts looked after her, you know. She'll witness that the old thing was fine until much more recently.'

'What about evidence from relatives, wouldn't that be more convincing?' Esmond said mildly.

'There was only the niece, and she's disappeared for the time being. Oh, no doubt she'll turn up,' Roger added. 'But she hadn't been down for years. Not a very welcome visitor, apparently. At least, that's what I've heard.'

'And the owner went mad later, is that it?'

'Yes, that's right. But my aunt will prove it was within the last few years.'

'What about the doctor, for instance, and the lawyers?' Esmond persisted.

'I'm the lawyer,' Bill said gloomily. 'Trouble is, I only took over the case when my father died and he always said the whole family was mad anyway. But I really can't discuss it now – I shall have to go. I'm sorry, Thea. Randall, Roger, you'll have to get another firm to represent you. This is all very embarrassing, very distressing,' and he went away rubbing his hands like the White Rabbit.

'As for the doctor,' Roger said with a hint of triumph in his voice, 'she never had a thing wrong with her physically. He only went there once in ten years, that my aunt could remember, when the old lady had a verrucha or something. Of course the niece tried to interfere, get her certified and so on: would have meant money to her, I expect. But they stopped that. She wasn't violent, you know. Just gently out of her mind. It would be hard to tell when the dividing line between madness and sanity came, in her case.'

'Yes, she was always an individual,' Randall confirmed. 'When I first came down here, just after the war it would have been, she was behaving like royalty, driving round in some old horse drawn carriage and patronising the locals. But that's only eccentricity, not madness.' Esmond was not making notes, but Thea knew men like him and Sylvester well enough to be sure that he would not forget a syllable of all this. She hated this unseemly wrangling. It all seemed hideously removed from the true meaning of the find, the implications to scholarship and discovery; and even perhaps, though it meant less to her, the lonely resting place of a long – dead grandee; all this felt far more like desecration than the actual disinterment of his bones.

'Fortunately I can confirm that,' Roger said rapidly. 'I lived near there as a boy, and as I say my family worked at Pentowan. There weren't any flies on Miss Trevanion.'

'There, you see, home and dry,' Randall declared. 'Don't suppose Bill will even bring it to court, without the old Ferris girl there to make him. A lovely untaxed windfall.'

'You don't feel that in a way it's – er – stealing, to take over land like that?' Esmond inquired delicately.

'Not unless all property is theft, I don't,' Randall said. 'And I'm a good capitalist. You can put that in your article if you like. Everyone that knows me knows that. No, what the law allows me, is mine. And half to Roger, in this case. So that's all hotsy totsy.' He stood up, and patted Thea familiarly on the shoulder. 'All turned out very nicely, wouldn't you say? Well, I must be off. You can quote me if you like, Smith. I'll not be denying anything. So long.'

Esmond had an expression on his face which, different as

his features were from Sylvester's, reminded Thea of the interviewer in depth whom she knew best poised to strike. His voice was mild though, as he said to Roger, 'Well, that seems to work out nicely for you. You and your relatives swear that Miss Trevanion was sane twelve years ago, and in exchange Randall Cooper shares the proceeds of the find with you.' Roger leapt up on to his feet. 'You make it sound as though we've made some shady deal!' he exclaimed.

'One might say, if the cap fits, put it on,' Esmond murmured. 'But no, I didn't imply that, in fact. It was a straight comment. But presumably you'd get no financial benefit if Mr Cooper lost his case. The law doesn't say Finder's Keeper's, does it?'

'Only if the true owner is unknown and undiscoverable,' Thea said slowly. This aspect of the relationship between Randall and Roger had not occurred to her before, but seemed hideously plausible now, knowing Roger's personal ambition and Randall's commercial ruthlessness of which he boasted himself. 'But the law generally is that the landowner is entitled to property found on his land, no matter who finds it. Except in the case of treasure trove, and that's only objects made of precious metals.'

'So aren't you lucky, Mr Thurstan? I really mean it – don't look so angry with me. The find of a lifetime for an archaeologist. I'd very much like to see the site, if I may. Would you consider taking me over there after lunch? I don't know whether I'm allowed to buy it for you here, but we could go down to the Grand Hotel if you'd care to.' When Esmond was nice he was very very nice, Thea thought, like the little girl with the little curl in the middle of her forehead. She watched him charming the sulky young man into chatting and even laughing as they ate their mediocre luncheon in the Staff Club. After brandies all round, Roger said cheerfully, 'I'll just ring Celia to say that I'll be home later. We can go over to Pentowan in my car; are you coming, Thea?'

'Yes, I'd like to. Let's just go over to the department, you can telephone from there and I'll pick up my letters.' Thea was mellowed too, she realised, as she went into the tall building unhindered by qualms about the perceptible swaying in the wind. It must be gale force by now. The decorative campus trees were tossing as though they were in some galactic tumbler, and a fallen tree lay right across the front lawn and herbaceous border. It had not rained for several days, and Thea put on sunglasses to protect her eyes from the dust as they walked across from the staff club, only to find that eddies blew specks over and under their frames into her eyes just the same. It was so noisy in the building that they were obliged almost to shout. In the rooms, draughts blew through the ventilators, and a pile of Thea's papers was scattered on the floor. 'Oh, don't bother, Esmond,' she said, as he stooped to pick them up. 'They are only circulars. Just let me look here...' Mrs Tobias had weighted several piles of mail already sorted on Thea's desk, and there were a couple of parcels. Roger came in looking hang dog after talking to his wife as Thea said, 'Oh look, this is from the Conservation Labs. It may be the cross back – I'll just open it a minute if you'll wait.' She slit the sealed and blue pencilled paper, and unwrapped from several layers the familiar object. It was glossy now, and all the figures on it stood out in sharp relief. The Conservation Laboratories had made a lovely job of it, she thought: every crevice cleaned, and the whole preserved for eternity with modern chemicals.

Roger held out his hand. 'I'm glad to have it back,' he said.

'But – do you want to take it now?' Thea was reluctant to give it to him. 'Shouldn't it be locked up or something? I hardly like . . .'

'It's more his than yours,' Esmond said with an amused smile, 'And didn't you say that you didn't care about its financial value?'

'I'll take good care of it, don't worry,' Roger said, but he wrapped it in tissue paper irreverently, and put it in the breast pocket of his jacket. 'I've got to draw it, and make measurements, and all that,' he said.

'I know,' Thea answered. It was true; and what harm could come to it in the hands of its excavator? Yet she felt unhappy to think that it was not safely in some vault.

'Let's go, shall we?' she said.

'Oh Lord,' said Roger. 'I can't, I'm afraid. I rang Celia and she needs me to look after the baby. And she wants the car. I'm terribly sorry.' Thea regarded his abject expression coldly and then said,

'Very well. I'll take Mr Smith, I think, even if you can't come. What a pity.'

But she spoke less guardedly to Esmond as they went out to her Mini. She was nothing but scornful of her subordinate, and Esmond seemed to find it amusing that she, the feminist, should so resent the self assertion of the woman in Roger Thurstan's life, and his surrender to it.

The wind caught capriciously against the car, even in the narrow hedge-lined roads, and Thea felt anxious about her own ability to control it. But they reached the north coast safely, though Thea's nervousness was aggravated by the sight of a furniture van blown over by the wind on Hayle causeway. The wind gusting across the mud flats of the estuary had buffeted at right angles against the huge pantechnicon's side, and as they watched the whole thing keeled majestically and slowly over like a wounded elephant. There was no need to stop, however, for the driver climbed calmly out of the cab, and stood looking at his vehicle as it lay in the ditch with a rueful smile; he was given a lift on a milk float into the town, apparently none the worse. Esmond said,

'It's always happening on motorways, even when the wind isn't gale force. Top-heavy great things. Don't worry, Thea: cars are better balanced.' And certainly, although Thea hypersensitively felt every sway and swerve of the wheels, they arrived without incident at Pentowan.

The wind was coming straight off the sea now, and as they turned off the main road on to the track leading to the excavations, a mixture of sand and spray clattered against the windscreen. There was already a thin layer of sand covering the ruts of the lane, and it was piled in little mounds against each fence post. One could see how the wind was stripping the dry sand away from the dunes, and the tufts of marram grass which were supposed to anchor them were being almost pressed into the ground. There was a patch of comparative shelter in the hollow where she parked the car, but even there it was necessary to get out of the car on the side away from the sea, and as Thea stood upright she felt sand raining against her face like shot-gun pellets. She tied her chiffon scarf over her face like a mask, but it obscured vision too much, and she decided rather to endure the painful whip-like sensation. She screwed her eyes tightly up, and kept her face aimed downwards. On other visits here she had mostly been admiring the view; but now she looked for the first time in detail at the multitudes of miniature flowers that grew on the sand, so small that she had not noticed them before, though in their perfection of shape and colour they were well worth the seeing.

She missed the sound of the larks and the smell of the wild thyme though. It was too dry for the latter, and nothing could be heard above the wind except the pattering of the sand on to her hard plastic coat.

They climbed, bent double, up the steep dune to the excavation, and skated down the other side leaning against a wall of wind. The sea was malachite green, with gigantic breakers and waves white-striping it, and though it was only half tide the spray reached up to the top of the cliffs. Thea rushed for the shelter of the end of the little boat-house, and stood leaning against it for a rest. Now that she could safely open her eyes she saw that the ragged pits and holes which had been there on her last visit had been much changed, though it was not clear whether by human or boreal effort. It all looked like a beach where children have been playing for a long summer day, and on which the waves are just licking: as though castles and causeways were beginning to be flattened by the impartial water. There were now neither trenches nor dumps, but smooth humps and hollows in the ground, and there was a visible veil of flying sand above it, as the wind gouged at the protuberances and filled in the holes. Thea found a passage of music from Messiah running through her mind: 'Every valley shall be exalted and every mountain and hill made low; the crooked straight and the rough places plain.'

Esmond Smith came and stood beside her and smiled when he heard what she was humming. He said,

'Not much like your digs now, is it?'

'It never was,' Thea answered tartly. 'But I must say that on any other site I'd find this heartbreaking. Here there wasn't much left to spoil. Don't print it, but you can't imagine what a mess this place was even before the vandals got at it.'

'Not a good archaeologist then, our handsome young friend?'

Thea could not bring herself to answer in words, but her silence was eloquent. Esmond lit his pipe.

'Look how the wind catches every tiny inch that sticks up,' he said. 'Do you see how it's shifting the whole land surface? Fascinating to watch. I've never seen anything like it.'

'They say locally that a whole village was overwhelmed by the sand in one night. And it reappears and gets reburied every century or so.'

'Remarkable. It's so easy to think of Cornwall as nothing but sunshine and clotted cream. One forgets about storms and wreckers and this sort of thing.'

'Well, no doubt you'll remind your readers. I can't say I like this much. Let's go and see if Rose Ferris is back.'

They drove around to Pentowan House. It was withstanding this, as many previous gales, and the one advantage of the concrete which surrounded it was that there was nothing to uproot. Thea rang the front door bell, and soon there were footsteps clattering along the tiled passage. 'She's back!' Thea said, but the door was opened by the middle-aged maid who had been there once on one of Thea's previous calls.

'Oh, good afternoon; Maud, isn't it? Is Miss Ferris home yet?'

'Good afternoon, madam. No, that she's not. I only came up myself just to see if she was all right, couldn't sit happy at home for wondering, after all she's nothing to me, only I was here with her old aunt for such a long time. But she hasn't come back at all. So I thought I'd better have a look at the house, you get to feel responsible, don't you, madam, after all those years, come in, madam, do, and you, sir, that's right, come in here, used to be the smoking-room when the old gentleman was alive this did, but then we had to call it the chapel, never could remember, always be the smoking-room to me it will. Well, madam, as I was saying, Miss Ferris is still away but that sneaking Batty's been here, he ran out the back as I rang the front bell and that's how I got in. I gave in my keys when I left, I need hardly tell you that, but he's hung on to his way of getting in, wretch that he is. So I thought I'd better just have a look around. Oh, the sand's something terrible, always has been here, but now, all that wind after the dry spell, well it's like as if I'd spilt twenty bags of sugar in the house. Not that it's my duty, but I thought I'd sweep up a little, can't bear to see it after I kept it so nice all these years, break your heart, it would.'

Thea had a sudden realisation of how the sites she uncovered became inhumed over the centuries. Even in this well-built house there was, as Maud said, sand everywhere, coming in through infinitesimal crannies. There were layers of it on all the flat surfaces. It wouldn't take so many years for the house to be completely silted up in this way: and if it went on, in perhaps as little as fifty years here would stand not a four-square granite mansion but another huge sand dune, smooth curved and mysterious.

Maud had bustled away for the boom like Mrs Tittlemouse. 'It still smells of incense,' Esmond said.

'Incense?' Thea said sharply.

'Mm, she said it was used as a chapel. Here's a whole cupboard full of holy objects – can she have been a Roman Catholic? And look, this is a lovely bit of embroidery. An altar cloth, would you say?' He continued wandering around the room, hands in pockets. 'Look,' he said, peering sideways at the wall. 'Here's a faded patch. Cross-shaped, I think. There must have been a prie-dieu underneath.' Thea examined the grey brocade paper. It was indeed just visible that a cross had been hung there.

'Esmond, do you realise that it's exactly the shape and size of the ivory? What an extraordinary – I was going to say coincidence,' she ended her sentence slowly. 'Did I tell you about the incense resins that Helmuth Muller found in the cross?' she said, and when he said that she had not, explained about it.

They stood in silence looking at the shadow on the wall. He's like a catalyst to my mind, Thea thought. Just because he's so unassertive, he listens like a psychiatrist and I say things which I'm not aware of having thought. Maud came into the room, sweeping busily, with a small hard brush, her bottom raised roundly towards the ceiling as she backed out of the hall. She straightened up with a ritual groan.

'Me poor bones, couldn't do this often any more. I've got a nice upright vacuum cleaner at my cottage, saves all this bending, though I will say I managed it for years. You're looking at the place where Miss Victoria used to pray, kneeling there for hours every day she was, that'll be some time back now. I see Miss Rose moved the little kneeling table upstairs, can't say I blame her, religion's all very well in its own place, though I'm Chapel and always have been. And I wouldn't like to say what's happened to the cross, not that I haven't got a very good idea. I can tell you, light-fingered that he always was, like his whole family.'

'Who, Maud?' asked Thea.

'Why Batty Phillips, who else, came in here he did. I'm as certain as if I'd seen him do it myself, helped himself to a pocket full of things after the place was empty. I told the lawyer gentleman from Buriton, the place isn't safe, I said, but did he take any notice, no, not a bit of it. But I know that the cross was there when Miss Victoria died because Emmy wanted to put in on her chest when we laid her out and I said no, Emmy I said, nasty heathen thing with all that messy carving, graven images, that's what it was, not on my Miss Victoria that's been like a holy innocent all these years. And then I came to collect my things, they'd mounted up over all this time, you know how it is, madam, that nephew of mine that's done so well for himself, he came to help me carry everything, and I just went round, to say goodbye as you might say, before shutting the front door behind me, well I'd worked here for ever such a long time, madam, started as a kitchen maid when I wasn't but a girl, well I thought I deserved a final farewell, don't you think so, madam?'

'And the cross was gone, then?'

'Clean gone, I saw the patch on the wall straight away, angry, I could have stamped my feet, I wanted to get the police on the unchristian creature, nasty verminous thing, but my nephew, he said there weren't no point, not just for a thing like that. So I left it. Well, what can you do, madam, the family had always encouraged that lot, no matter what I'd say, I suppose they'd have turned in their graves if I'd set the police on to him now. Not that he hasn't lived off them, poaching and pinching. I hope Miss Rose will send him to the right-about when she gets back, it'll be no more than he deserves.'

'Poor Miss Trevanion,' Thea said, forcing her voice to concern. 'She was out of her mind, was she, for years?'

'Well, madam, Emmy and me, we used to say she wasn't exactly out of her mind, just being in her own mind when she was a child that's all. Didn't do any harm to a living soul, so good and obedient she was, we fair loved her for all the village said she was crazy. It was such a change from what she'd been before, ever so dignified she was till the last years, a real lady of the old school, if you know what I mean, madam. But then she just went backwards in time, as you might say.'

'How long was she like that?'

'Oh, it must have been fifteen years or so—' Maud clapped her red hand over her mouth and stared at them above it with horrified eyes. 'What am I saying? I know what it is, madam, the years went by so slow, all the same they seemed, only told the seasons changing here by the cold, no flowers in the garden as you'll have noticed, madam and sir, the days just slip by uncounted as you might say. No, I tell a lie, I'm afraid, I was talking about it the other day to Emmy, we was working it out, can't have been more than five or six years that she was like that, poor lady. About half a dozen. And now, madam, if you'll excuse me I must be getting back to the village. I'll lock the door after us, that's right, though it's wasted effort for all the good it'll do with that Batty about, but there we are, what can you do? Good day, madam, good day, sir,' and she tripped off down the drive on small pointed feet, with her maroon felt hat bobbing up and down into the distance.

Esmond insisted on giving Thea dinner at the Grand Hotel in Buriton before catching the night train. He was agreeable and undemanding company, and it was not until she had been talking to him for a long time that Thea realised that he was treating her as he did his interview subjects. He deliberately played down his own personality, she thought, so that the people to whom he was speaking would display theirs, and his air of impersonal detachment encouraged indiscretions. She found herself telling him all about Rose Ferris's disappearance again, and about the crucifix and Helen Eliot and everything else that had happened since she came to Buriton. She mentioned Bill Nankervis's anxieties too, but Esmond had heard about Randall's claim to the land in the Staff Club and she skated round mentioning him, while being uneasily aware that Esmond was shrewd enough to guess why.

It was irritating to think that Sylvester might have sent Esmond down to find out what was going on; yet when she told all these things in their order they sounded far more sinister than she intended. And, somehow, there seemed to be some connection between events which had hitherto seemed unrelated. When Esmond said lightly,

'Goodness, what a chain of dramas, in only three weeks,' she replied:

'Oh nonsense, it's all coincidence.'

'Are you sure? Sylvester wasn't. One woman dies, another disappears, and an ambitious young man makes his fortune with one scrape of your son's trowel. You've got high standards if you think it's every day life.' Thea laughed, and Esmond blew smoke rings from his placid pink face, but she felt that he meant what he said; and after she had seen him into his sleeping compartment, she stood indecisively on the platform, wondering what to do. Somehow, the very act of marshalling her thoughts into speech had clarified them, and she was uncomfortably aware of discrepancies that she had not noticed earlier. Not, she told herself, that any of this really concerned her. And yet, it might just be worth going in to the university library on the way home and checking on one detail that she had not thought to mention to Esmond. That green stain on the Victoria and Albert Museum *Bulletin* was worrying her: for now she remembered where she had seen something similar. Would two bottles of green ink, of all colours, have been spilt in Buriton recently? And if not, that meant that the *Bulletin* had been looked at – she checked her thoughts, chiding herself for theorising before getting enough data. But it was worth just having another look.

XIII

The janitor was not at his desk when Thea went into the library, and she walked briskly up to the fourth floor, too preoccupied to be worried by the dark, silent alcoves and corridors. The only sound was of her shoes creaking, and the swing doors closing behind her as she went from room to room.

The lights were on in the Art History and Archaeology section, and as Thea went into it she caught sight of her own reflection in one of the windows; a small, thin hurrying figure, looking strangely insubstantial with the scudding moonlit clouds behind it.

She turned into the narrow passage between bookcases where the journals she wanted were housed. They were, as she had remembered, on the bottom shelf, and she dragged a stool over to crouch on. As she did so, there was a dull click from the door, and she leapt up, remembering too late the electric locks: that must be why the janitor was not at his desk, he must have been going round the library to make sure that all the readers had left, and by some extraordinary mischance she had missed him on the way up here. With automatic adult calm, she told herself that there were worse places to be stuck for the night than a library, and at least there was nobody at home to worry about her. And then there was a footstep behind her, and a voice said, in the words of the old horror story,

'And now we're locked in together for the night.'

Thea spun around, dropping the bound volume she was

holding, and stared up at Roger Thurstan. There was a grin fixed on his pale face, and he put up his hands to clutch her by the shoulders. The surprise of seeing him was such that Thea was frightened, but only briefly. Then she laughed and said,

'Oh, Roger, have you got caught in here too? Isn't it silly? What happens, will a night-watchman come round later and let us out?'

He did not answer, but stared down at her face. It was utterly quiet in the room, barricaded from the outside world as it was by rows of locked baize doors. Then came the sound of a train, borne up from sea level by the wind, and Thea thought of Esmond stretching himself out for the night, and she remembered why she had come to the library in the first place. She glanced down at the spread-eagled book she had dropped on the floor. It had fallen open at the number of the Victoria and Albert Museum *Bulletin* she had looked at with Randall. The clip holding journals inside their binding had burst, and Roger bent slowly down and picked it up. The green ink jumped startlingly in her vision.

'Is this what you came for?' he said.

'Yes.'

'Why?'

'I wondered if it was you that spilt the ink,' she said, her words tinkling in the silence. He sat down suddenly on the low stool and buried his face in his long, bony hands. He said in a muffled voice,

'I knew I'd never get away with it really.' Thea sat down on the floor beside him. Her fingers automatically stroked the smooth shiny paper. She said gently,

'I saw the same coloured stain in your house, you see. Tell me about it. It's the ivory cross, isn't it? You knew it was there all along?' He paused before answering, and then said in a hoarse, laboured voice,

'Oh Christ, I put the bloody thing there. Of course I knew. I planted it, sank it, salted the site. But you know that – why ask?'

'I didn't know it. I was just beginning to wonder.'

'Was this the only mistake I made?' he asked, pointing at the ink stained paper. 'It was Henry, he knocked over the bottle. He'd only just learned to crawl, I hadn't noticed he was so mobile. How was I to know you'd come snooping here? I'd have destroyed this long before.'

'What made you think of it today?' she said.

'Randall told me this morning how you'd shown him what the Victoria and Albert ivory fetched. But I couldn't come before. Celia was out with the car until late, and I had to stay with Henry. Anyway, I couldn't have known that you'd come and look this evening. It's not proof of anything. Just because I happened to have been reading about something similar.'

'No, but it makes one think. It must have been you that took the crucifix from Pentowan House, when you went there with your aunt. I suppose you recognised it. I saw the mark on the wall where it used to hang.'

'It's not everyone that would have recognised it,' he said huffily. 'It takes a trained mind. But I couldn't know its value. And there was no point in the whole business unless it was worth a lot. I couldn't believe my luck.'

'How did you manage to plant it so neatly?' she asked.

'I told you, I'm an archaeologist. I knew that it was a chapel site with burials. I'm not falsifying knowledge, I have a professional conscience too you know. The thing probably came from there in the first place. Batty Phillips was always bringing in things like bits of human bone that the rabbits had turned up in that bit of the sand dunes.

That's almost certainly where the Trevanions got it in the first place. All I was doing was putting it back where it came from.'

'You managed it very neatly.'

'Yes, didn't I? It was quite easy, you know. I got the idea from an article about American universities where they train their students entirely on digs they've salted with finds. In *Antiquity*, it was. Not that the terrain didn't help, I admit. It's quite easy with sand. I blew it about with a pair of bellows, you know. And of course it was getting dark when we unearthed it again.'

'Why did you do it, Roger? Wouldn't publishing it as a lost early crucifix have been enough? And the site would have been worth the digging, anyway.'

'You'll never understand, someone like you. I deserve the publicity just as much as anyone else does, I'd be as good at broadcasting and doing the television series. I'd make as good a professor as you. But it's a vicious circle, you don't get anywhere till you've made a name and you can't make a name until you've arrived. It's the security, you wouldn't know about that, but I've got a family to provide for, there's Henry, and Celia. But I should have known that fate would be against me. If it wasn't one thing it would have been another. When I saw you this evening I knew I was done for, it wasn't worth trying to brazen it out. So *now* what are you going to do about it?'

They stood facing one another, and Thea dropped her eyes from Roger's stare. He put his hands against the book-case, behind her head, and his arms on either side of her shoulders. He smelt, faintly and sourly, of sweat. He was a narrow man, flimsy despite his height; she felt sorry for him, fraudulent as he was. He hadn't broken the law. A person like Randall Cooper would not even know what she was worried about, the protests of her academic conscience would seem to him like a baroque joke. He must in fact have known about the fraud, she realised. He stood to lose or gain so much money. There had presumably been a bargain: the maid would be persuaded to lie about the period of Miss Trevanion's madness if Roger could have half shares in what the cross fetched. And what, a voice inside her whispered, was wrong with that? No person would suffer by it, and only a footnote of learning would be different.

And so what about Miss Ferris? But the thing had never really belonged to her anyway. And the only other person who might have guessed the truth was dead: poor Miss Eliot.

Roger was standing motionless, his chin a little above Thea's bent head, his breathing heavy. She accused herself – it's only because he's an attractive man you're hesitating. You wouldn't if he were old and ugly. Miss Eliot would have been ruled by her scholarly scruples all right.

A clear picture sprang into her mind, of Helen Eliot turning a trusting back to Roger, reading aloud to him with innocent pleasure the Latin description of the very cross he had claimed to unearth from a thousand years of burial. If he had picked the fender up bodily and swung it against her head ... He might even have burnt that folder; the original source had been destroyed during the war, Miss Eliot had said so. He'd be safe in thinking that nobody else knew about it.

Thea must have involuntarily stiffened at the thought. Roger stood a little away from her, and his hands moved closer together, until they rested on the slope of her skin where neck and shoulders join. She stood absolutely still, as one would if a fierce dog were sniffing at ones ankles, and forced herself to breathe regularly. Nobody would hear her if she screamed.

And yet, how ridiculous to imagine that Roger was dangerous. A more ineffectual man she had yet to meet – outside a place where they were, as he had said, locked in together for the night.

He gazed down at her, fractionally tightening his grip, and suddenly sprang away. There were heavy footsteps coming towards the room, and then the door opened. The janitor's comfortable Cornish voice called, 'Anyone there, is there?' and Thea said loudly,

'Oh, thank you so much. Yes, we were locked in.' She walked quickly down the aisle of books, and Roger followed her. She said smiling, 'I was afraid.'

'Afraid of spending the night here, were you? I'm not surprised. We do warn the readers about the electric locks, miss, at the door. But I saw there were cars still outside, so I came to make sure. After you, miss, after you, sir. I'll just turn the lights out as we go.'

Thea drove away without giving Roger a chance to speak to her and told the porter at Barbican that she was not at home to visitors; to make certain, she bolted the door of her flat.

She still did not feel sure what Roger had been about to do, when the janitor mercifully interrupted him; had he planned to embrace or strangle her? She might have let him make love to her, at that. Perversely, the thought of fraudulent Roger was now less revolting than that of fascist Randall. But could he really have meant to hurt her? Surely that was incredible. Life just couldn't be like that, no matter what Esmond and Sylvester might think.

XIV

Thea was woken at ten the next morning from a drugged sleep. It was Polly Nankervis on the telephone, her normally languid voice higher pitched and panting.

'Listen, there's something terrifically exciting going on over at Pentowan,' she began. Thea screwed up and blinked her eyes trying to clear her vision. The outside world looked blurred and she was a little dizzy after too many barbiturates taken in despair in the small hours. But she could see that, unpredictable to the last, the wind had completely dropped, and a mild sunshine sparkled on the mortuary of vegetation in the college garden below. Thea unstuck her tongue from the sandpapery roof of her mouth and tried to concentrate on what Polly was chattering about. Bill had been telephoned by Maud, the former Pentowan maid, and had dashed off in the car, without a by your leave, Polly said. 'He didn't even ask whether I needed it today, and he simply wouldn't tell me what was wrong. He just muttered something about it being unsuitable – and if there's one thing I just can't bear— So I thought we might go over together, Thea, in your Mini.'

'What's it all about?' Thea croaked.

'That's just it, I don't know. Though the poor woman sounded terribly agitated. I answered the telephone on our side of the house, you see, but it cuts out when I switch it through. Bill doesn't trust me not to listen in to his clients. Anyway, Thea, will you come? Surely you'd like to know what's going on?'

'What about the children?'

'Oh, the *au pair*'s here today. It's a gorgeous day, just right for a trip – and wouldn't you like to know what it's all about? She said she'd already tried to ring her nephew, that's Roger Thurstan. Do you think it's something to do with Rose Ferris turning up or something?'

Thea was intrigued herself, though she would have hesitated to rush over to rubberneck unless Polly had insisted. But as Polly had said, it was no hardship to go out on this lovely day, and some fresh air was really what she needed after yesterday. So Thea gulped down black coffee and picked up Polly not much later than she had said she would.

There were no cars parked outside Pentowan house itself, so they turned and went round to the cliff road, and found several empty cars in the usual place, including Bill Nankervis's. The shape of the sandhills had become completely unfamiliar. Where there had been foot-high tufts of marram grass, now only their sharp tips showed above the thickly blown sand and in some places it looked as though the dunes had shifted completely by several feet. None of the tiny flowers were left uncovered, and the soft yellow grains slithered and slipped under their feet as they walked. The air was balmy and soft, though there was still a tremendous swell out to sea and the tide crashed against the foot of the cliffs, and seagulls screamed and swooped above them.

The two women panted to the top of the dune, and paused astonished at what lay below. It was as though a gigantic trenching tool had swung across the hollow, scraping sand and turf from the surface and piling it against the landward walls. The boat-house was completely buried, only the black tube of its chimney poking out.

The whole area of the chapel was stripped, and its walls lay revealed, roughly rectangular, made of slates and beach pebbles married mortarless together, rising to about two feet above the mud coloured sub soil.

The wind had revealed the hollows of several graves, catching under every protuberance and scattering any loose soil. Some were still lined with small slate slabs, though the bones had been flung far and wide. Among the other six by two feet depressions, Thea did not at first notice that one was different from the others. When she looked in the direction, behind the mound of sand covering the hut, of where 'James's pit' had been, there was an immediate sensation of *déjà vu*', meaningless at first and then appalling. For there were people digging there, heaving away at the sand with long handled Cornish shovels, and then scraping delicately with the sharp edges of the tools. There was already a deep hole, which must mostly have been excavated by the wind; and as the two women approached they saw that it was a wide depression surrounding the place where there had been the narrow slit trench. In the centre of it, protruding from the soil and encrusted with damp sand, was what looked at first like a tweed blanket. As they watched, one of the uniformed policemen who were digging poked at the cloth with his foot and something blackened and stinking was revealed.

Polly gagged, and clapped her hand over her mouth. Bill Nankervis swung around furiously and shouted,

'My God, what the hell are you doing here? It's no place for women! Go away, go away,' and obediently Polly retreated to the dune, where she sat on the ground with her face between her knees. Thea watched more calmly as the work continued. It had been clear from the beginning that this was a human body, and if she could avoid breathing through her nose it was, to her, more interesting than revolting. One of the policemen snapped,

'Keep that damned animal away,' and a thin mongrel which was sniffing at his feet was hauled back by someone standing behind Thea. This was an elderly man who had come silently up, without her noticing, though if she had not been so carefully suppressing her sense of smell she might have become aware of him without hearing his footsteps. He pulled some twine from his pocket and tied it around the dog's neck. He grinned at Thea, with huge square false teeth, and said huskily,

'I found her, I did. 'Smorning, when I come rabbiting with Lassie here. See the walls, do ee? Always knew there was a village here right enough, I did. Told young Roger so many a time, for all he's too powerful smart to notice the likes of me, him and his auntie. Not like her, poor lady. Remember her when she weren't no moren' a kiddie.'

'Who is it?' Thea said in a low voice, though she knew the answer.

'That's Miss Rose, that is. Had a look, I did, before I covered her up a bit decent like, against they seagulls. Took 'em time enough to get here, the coppers.'

Bill Nankervis stepped back to stand beside Thea. His horrified eyes were fixed on the mouldering form now being uncovered, but he held a pad of handkerchief over his nose and mouth. He said,

'Mr Phillips used the telephone at Miss Tyack's cottage. That was why she got in touch with me. But I'm sorry Polly made you come. It's quite unsuitable.'

'I can take it,' Thea said drily, and did not add that she could probably take it better than Bill. But he was certainly a very delicate man, she thought. Though admittedly, her own reactions had been hardened in her younger days, when she had a medical student boy-friend who wanted to specialise in pathology, and insisted on showing her what he regarded as the glories of his subject.

The still-braided hair showed that the body was really that of Rose Ferris, and Thea was able to tell the policeman so. It would not have been possible to recognise anybody from the ruin of a face which lay revealed.

One of the policemen was about to cover the whole thing with a tarpaulin, when the other exclaimed, and picked something out of the trench; only its nozzle had been seen by his sharp eyes, but he pulled it out, holding it in a polythene gloved hand. He stood shaking the sand gently off it, and turned round to face Bill and Thea to show them what he had found. It was a pair of leather bellows, decorated with beading and poker work on the handles. Thea started to exclaim,

'But Roger said he —' when a drawling American voice came from the approach path. Celia Thurstan was coming towards them with her child seated in a canvas sling on her hip, and she was followed by Randall Cooper. Her view of the trench and its contents was blocked, but she said,

'Those bellows are mine: were did you get them? I was looking for them everywhere.'

Polly sprang up and seized Celia's arm, as Bill and Thea simultaneously shouted, 'Keep back.'

'What is all this?' she said petulantly. 'First some crazy dame calls up at crack of dawn to tell Roger to get over here, and then when I finally find someone to bring me as dear Roger hasn't been home all night I find a whole crowd standing round like the grave-diggers in Hamlet. What's going on round here?'

The young policeman put the bellows down on the tarpaulin and pulled off his polythene gloves. Then he deliberately put on his jacket. There were three stripes on the sleeve. He walked over to Celia.

'You recognise the bellows, do you, madam?' he asked.

'Of course I do. I got them in North Africa before I was married. What is all this, anyway?' She was standing slightly above him on the slope of the sand dune, and now that he had moved she could see over his head into the pit. Her eyes widened, but she said nothing, and it was Polly who grabbed the child from his mother and carried him well away. Suddenly a fountain of speech rose from Celia Thurstan.

'That's a body,' she cried. 'Did you find the bellows there? I knew it, I knew he'd make a God-darned fool of himself. Did he kill her? Did you find my bellows in there with her?'

'The bellows were buried in the same trench as the body, madam, yes. And it certainly seems to be a case of foul play. I must ask you not to approach any nearer. The cranium appears to have been struck by a heavy instrument.'

'I knew it, I knew it, he makes a balls-up of anything he touches. She must have found him when he was burying the cross and the bloody fool killed her. Oh, it's too much, I'm not taking any more. I'm leaving, Hal and I are going back to the States. You can hang him for all I care.' Her eyes were glittering like small beach pebbles still wet from the retreating sea. The policeman seemed to be astonished into silence. Thea said,

'Do you mean to say you knew about Roger planting the crucifix?'

'Naturally I did. He couldn't think of a scheme like that. Not in the necessary detail, he's a dreamer, a muddler, a bloody failure. What a fool, to think he could get away with this. What was the point of it?'

Thea was unsuitably racked with pity for this virago's husband. She said painfully, 'He only did it for you, and the baby. He wanted to give you security.'

'I didn't want security, you're not safe until you are dead. I wanted life. Not the living death he condemned me to, stuck here with the baby. Oh well.' She actually smiled. 'He can't provide much security from death row, I guess. I'll be lumbered with the kid, but I'm off. I'll wait in the car, Randall.' She snatched her wailing son from Polly's arms, and stumped off up the dune. Her audience looked, stunned, at one another. The sergeant slowly took his notebook and pencil from his pocket, and looked, man to man, at Bill. He said in an awed voice,

'I'd better take that down, sir. Who exactly was that lady?'

Bill was about to answer when a shout came from Randall, and he pointed up at the dune on the Pentowan House side of the sand pit. Roger Thurstan was walking towards them. From where he stood he could not see down into the hideous grave, and he called,

'Hullo, Randall, Thea. What's going on? There was a message at home that my Aunt Maud wanted me at Pentowan, but there's nobody at the house.' They stared as he came downhill towards them. And then he looked towards what had been James's pit, and stopped. 'So that's it,' he said slowly. He looked over towards the man in uniform; 'Don't worry, I'll come quietly. I know when I'm beaten. I always am.' The policeman looked astonished, but he was a quick-witted man, and he walked towards Roger swinging his hips like the sheriff in a western, about to arrest the bad guy. Randall said, too loudly,

'Well, I suppose the ivory's still worth something to someone.' But Roger grimaced and momentarily bared his teeth. He shouted,

'There are limits,' and in a quick movement withdrew his

hand from his pocket. The policeman sprang forward, showing courage since he must have expected a weapon to be in Roger's hand. But he was holding the little cross. He looked at it briefly, and then with an overarm swing of his arm, threw it as far as he could over the edge of the cliff. It was high tide, and there must have been fathoms of water crashing and thundering in foaming waves just below. The ivory crucifix was, this time, irretrievably lost.

Roger came to stand between the two policemen. He said clearly,

'There's another offence to take into consideration, as well as this one here. I killed her with a spade, when she came spying on me that evening. It should have worked, you know. I couldn't have been expected to guess there'd be a freak wind, could I? You have to admit, it was a neat plan, to get the little boys to finish filling in her grave, the next day, and to fix it so that one of them found the crucifix. I had bad luck, as usual, it wasn't bad judgement. And you'd never have known that it was me that came and destroyed the site, so that nobody could interfere and query the sequence. I did it that night, when I was driving the baby around. He's a good little chap, he's grown out of crying really. I did it all for him, anyway.'

The police sergeant still looked astonished, but he was writing busily, and when Roger paused he murmured the usual caution. Roger said,

'All right, all right, I told you, I'm not denying it. I'm a born loser, don't you see?'

'You mentioned another offence, sir,' the man said. Bill said sharply, 'Roger, don't—' but Roger glanced at him, and answered wearily,

'What's the point? You know as well as I do that I've had it. Anyway, I never hit her. Helen Eliot, I mean. I might have done, she was trying to foul everything up. She knew the crucifix hadn't been buried all that time you see, she had a file about the bloody thing. All I wanted was the file, just to destroy her notes, that was all. I don't suppose I'd have hurt her. But she slipped, when I was taking it from her. If only she'd have let go sensibly. But there was that great pool of muck on the floor, and she banged her head on the fender. Well, I couldn't get anyone, could I? Who'd have believed me? All I could do was burn the file and get out fast. But she was old, due to die. I didn't feel badly about her.'

He was still talking when they led him, a policeman to each arm, up the steep dune. He was making speeches of self-justification, and proclaiming himself the underdog, as his voice faded into the distance.

Bill said, 'My God, I suppose he'll want me to represent him,' but Polly linked her arm in his. 'There'll be nothing for counsel to do but make a plea in mitigation,' she said consolingly. 'Poor thing.'

Randall put his arm around Thea's shoulder, and it felt comforting and sane, and she let it stay. He said, 'Might keep this bit open as an ancient monument, even if Roger's aunt changes her evidence and I have to buy the plot, Bill. I'm told they draw the tourists. Must be practical,' he added.

Thea's mind had already escaped from the melodramas of real life. It may have been a defence mechanism, she diagnosed that even as she thought, but she was already turning over in her mind the opening sentences of an article on the lost Pentowan Ivory Cross. After all, who else was there to write it up now?